Bethany Rutter is a journalist and blogger who writes about fat bodies, plus size fashion and body politics including the benefits and limitations of body positivity. She works in marketing at a plus-size fashion brand and is an occasional DJ. Her writing has appeared in the *Guardian*, *Telegraph Magazine*, *Vogue*, *Dazed*, *RedOnline*, *The Debrief* and others. She co-hosts the podcast What Page Are You On? and is the author of *Plus+*, a coffee table book offering style inspiration for everyone.

# NO BIG DEAL

## BETHANY RUTTER

MACMILLAN CHILDREN'S BOOKS

*For Julie and Jonathan*

First published 2019 by Macmillan Children's Books
an imprint of Pan Macmillan
20 New Wharf Road, London N1 9RR
Associated companies throughout the world
www.panmacmillan.com

ISBN 978-1-5098-7005-9

3 5 7 9 8 6 4 2

A CIP catalogue record for this book is available from
the British Library.

Printed and bound by CPI Group (UK) Ltd, Croydon CR0 4YY

# CHAPTER ONE

## 'Like a Virgin' – Madonna

'What's taking you so long?' Abi calls from outside the changing-room door.

I'd bet all the coins in my pocket that Abi's never got stuck in a dress at Topshop. Or maybe this is a thing that happens to really thin people too. I wouldn't know.

'Oh, nothing. I was just texting my dad, and I'm only just trying the dress on now.' I do my best to keep the laughter out of my voice, hoping someday soon I'll be able to wriggle out of this lilac polyester number. No matter how hard I pull, no matter how much I try to flatten my boobs, this dress is going nowhere.

'OK, bud – I'll go and look at shoes till you're done. The skirt was too big for me anyway,' she says.

Insult to injury.

I hear her clatter out of the changing room, and I'm alone, dripping with sweat, feeling ridiculous, trying to figure out how I got the dress over my shoulders and boobs in the first place. Surely science dictates that what goes on must come off again? Whatever the science, in this

1

scenario, there's only one thing for it. I must take decisive and dramatic action.

Carefully, slowly, imperceptibly I push the door open and peek outside. The changing room is still unattended, and in an empty changing room, no one can hear you pull a dress so hard over your head that you rip the seams.

So I do it.

The dress deserves it. The dress is now my arch-nemesis and needs to be punished. Jesus, what a close call. My arms are shaking from being stuck upright in the air for several minutes. I need a lie down. No more trying on clothes that will clearly never fit me.

I step back into my decidedly plus-size jeans (black, tight and artfully ripped), button up my leopard-print shirt, and slip on my sandals, before fleeing my minor crime scene and going to rejoin Abi and the others. Abi is eyeing up the highest heels on the shelf, picking them up and turning them over to check the price. Ella is trying on some holographic trainers, and Sophia, Ella's girlfriend, is holding her bag while closely examining the skin around her nails, apparently looking for the next finger to nibble on.

'No joy?' Abi asks.

'No – it was a bit too short,' I lie.

Abi shrugs as if to say, *It happens to us all*.

If Camila were here, I would probably confess my crime

to her in exchange for some sympathy, but she's still visiting her grandparents in Sweden. She'd understand, not just because she's the only other fat girl in my year at school, but also because she's my best friend. She gets me. She'll be home on Sunday, ready to start the new term, and I cannot wait to see her.

'Someone tell me I do not need holographic platform trainers,' says Ella, 'or I'll end up buying these, and Sophia will have to go without a birthday present.'

'No chance,' Sophia says, handing Ella's bag back, snaking an arm around her waist and kissing her.

They're completely obsessed with each other, and it's kind of perfect. Their relationship feels like looking into another world to me – a landscape I've never even set foot in. I am a seventeen-year-old romance-free zone. It just hasn't happened for me yet, and it's starting to worry me.

'Can we get out of here?' I'm still a little light-headed from overheating inside that too-tight dress and need to breathe the sweet Croydon air.

'Where to?' asks Abi.

'I'm in the mood for a milkshake,' says Sophia.

It's a foregone conclusion: we're already walking in that direction.

The four of us head up the escalator to Milkbar, Ella and Sophia blocking the way by refusing to let go of each other,

Abi furiously messaging, and me just trying to cool the hell down. When we arrive, we realize we are in luck: Priyanka is at work today. And Priyanka working at Milkbar means upgraded milkshakes.

'Priyanka, my sweet princess, love of my life, angel of my dreams!' says Abi, blowing kisses over the counter.

'Yes, you can have some free shit,' says Priyanka, clearly overjoyed to see us after a day of frazzled summer-holiday parents and their over-sugared children. She gets started on our usual orders.

Priyanka should not be left unattended; she's probably skimmed hundreds of pounds' worth of Jaffa Cakes, Maltesers, Oreos and chocolate flakes off the top of Milkbar's stock over the summer she's worked here – and that's just for us.

It's late August, all our summer obligations are over, and we've really run out of things to do: traipsing around the Whitgift Centre, trying on clothes we can't afford (or in my case, fit into), drinking milkshakes, lying on the grass in front of the civic centre. Croydon has limited options in terms of how to spend your summer holiday. And this is the last one that will end with a return to school. The last one with comfort and familiarity on the horizon. After this year, we'll all be going off to university, off to . . . well, who knows what?

'Voila,' says Priyanka, handing us our orders and ringing up a nominal amount on the till. 'Guess who was in here earlier?'

'We could be here a while,' I reply. 'Just tell us.'

'Ben,' she says, smiling and adjusting her uniform baseball cap.

'Was he alone or are the lads out and about?' Abi asks, twisting her braids into a bun on top of her head, trying to act like she doesn't care what the answer is.

'Yeah, a few of them were out, including Oliver – I know that's what you're actually asking – but I didn't really chat much to them. Ben was looking A plus plus, and that's all that matters.'

'You have to step it up,' says Abi. 'You literally have one year left to convert this crush into a reality before we all disappear for uni, and he is gone forever! Step on it!'

Abi is always passionately encouraging people to get it on. It's one of her talents.

'But I would literally cringe myself to death if I put myself out there, and he wasn't into me.' Priyanka is clearly in need of a pep talk.

'You already know, pretty much for definite, that he's into you,' I say. 'I think if any of us thought there was a chance he wasn't interested, we wouldn't be telling you to go for it.'

'You're right. You're always right. Less making milkshakes – more making out.' Priyanka nods sagely. Her face suddenly breaks into a big grin, and she twirls on the spot, too full of enthusiasm over the promise of Ben to stay still.

For someone with little (read *zero*) experience in matters of the heart (and the bedroom), it's surprising how often I'm called upon to bring a sense of rationality to a situation. But I really can't imagine being certain that someone was definitely into me. Bless Camila for being as useless as I am. We're sisters in arms in the barren land of No Romance. I miss her a lot. Two months is a long time to be apart from your best friend, and to make matters worse, she's in an internet-free zone. Turns out old Swedish people who live on tiny islands aren't that bothered about Wi-Fi.

Abi's right though: one year left until we're spat out into the real world, jumbled up with a new mix of people who don't know us. Do I really want to leave for uni without ever having so much as kissed anyone? Maybe I need to step on it too? Maybe now actually is the time?

'Guys . . . I know it's an integral part of my personal brand, but I'm bored of nothing ever happening for me,' I say.

'Happening like *how*?' asks Abi.

'Happening, like, with guys, I guess,' I reply, casting my

eyes downwards into the chocolatey mess of my milkshake. I'm suddenly embarrassed, like this isn't me – this isn't my stuff.

'Mate, it's fine. Don't worry about it – you have loads of time! Life is long, isn't it? You don't have to do everything right now,' Ella offers encouragingly.

'It's not about everything; it's about *anything*. I feel so far behind. And why would it ever change? If it hasn't happened by now, maybe it'll never happen.' I know I sound sulky, but it's a source of ever-increasing frustration to me. It doesn't make sense – I'm objectively a catch. I'm cute and fun and funny, I wear good clothes, and I feel like I've got pretty damn good at make-up after watching a thousand YouTube tutorials. What's going wrong?

'Honestly, you just have to go for it. You never put yourself out there. You never act like you're interested in anyone. Make it happen,' says Abi.

'Easy for you to say – guys literally trip over themselves trying to get with you,' I say. And I'm happy for her, but we are fundamentally different beasts. Abi is tall and slim, with long limbs always moisturized to perfection, long braids in an ever-rotating array of colours, and enormous brown eyes. She's a babe.

'I have to make an effort too,' Abi says, looking at me earnestly. 'I have to show I'm interested – give them a bit of encouragement, right? It doesn't just happen out of nowhere; it needs a bit of give and take. Just pick someone at Ben's party tomorrow night, make him your target, and see where you get. You're cute. No, you're really cute, you're fun, you're super clever, you're nice, and anyone would be lucky to get with you.'

'Word! I'd date you,' Ella says with a wink.

'You're all far too kind, but I'm going to choose to believe you on this occasion,' I say. I like me, my friends like me, how hard can it possibly be to get guys to like me?

We slurp in silence for a few moments. Relative silence. Milkbar's stereo is blasting the sound of the summer, the song we've heard in every shop and every cafe and coming out of every car radio at every set of traffic lights since at least May.

'Maybe it would help if you came to my dance class with me?' Ella ventures, out of nowhere.

I keep slurping. It's only when no one replies that I look up to see who she was talking to.

Everyone's looking at me.

'Oh, *me*? What? Why?' I look shiftily around the group, and then I realize why. 'Oh . . . you mean like a . . . like a weight-loss thing?'

Ella goes red and immediately starts babbling. 'No, no – I didn't mean . . . I just thought . . . maybe that was what you wanted? Like maybe that's what you were saying?'

'Ah, Jesus,' I say, shaking my head and grimacing. 'Let's never speak of this again.' I am not getting into a whole weight loss discussion *thing* today. And besides, that's not the problem . . . is it?

'No, no – you're right. It's cool. Sorry. I have every faith in your current project,' Ella says, reaching out a small, perfectly tanned hand and resting the back of it against my cheek for a second. It's a gentle act, and I feel it.

We chat as we finish our milkshakes, but I kind of zone out. I don't think I'm a lost cause; I just haven't tried hard enough. The more I think about it, the better I feel. Now is my time to shine, to take control of my own destiny. But as I sip my Malteser milkshake through the candy-striped straw, I struggle to think of a deserving target. I mentally go through a list of the boys I know: Abi is hooking up with Oliver; Priyanka has her eye on Ben; I think Fred is pretty cute, but mostly just really nice; Cameron likes football too much; Kenji is way too good-looking for me (or, it seems, anyone); and Tommy is permanently stoned, which is really not my scene.

It's not like they're the only guys in our year at Alexander Hall, or the only guys in Croydon, or the only guys in the world, but realistically, they're the ones we see the most. Maybe I need to broaden my horizons and actually talk to some people I don't know at Ben's party tomorrow night. Surely that's the very best possible place to start this mission . . .

I feel energized! Fizzing with possibilities. Furiously jubilant! I'm already excited for my future self, whenever she decides to make an appearance.

# CHAPTER TWO

'Don't Make Me Over' – Julia Holter

At home that night, I set my mind to the important task of figuring out what to wear to Ben's party.

My bedroom isn't the ideal place for me to figure out anything, really. I like having stuff. I find it comforting never getting rid of things, finding more and more nooks and crannies to push any new stuff into, which means my bedroom is always a bit of a bomb site. I have nothing else to spend my babysitting money on but clothes, so clothes are what I spend it on.

I pick my way across the floor, better known as the floordrobe, stripping down to my underwear in readiness to start trying on everything in my search for the ideal look. I toss my clothes on my bed and pick up the framed photo of Camila and me that lives on my bedside table. Two cute, smiling girls look back at me: one pale and freckly (that's me); the other sleek and tanned (that's her); both fat.

Camila's always been very open about wanting a boyfriend, wanting romance, wanting that kind of love. She's kind of a romantic – or at least, she's less of a cynic than I am. Come to think of it, we don't have that much in common. I'm loud; she's quiet. I'm abrasive; she's mild. I'm always leaving things to the last minute; she's a diligent planner. I'm into fashion; she doesn't care what she wears as long as it doesn't draw attention to her. We've been friends for a really long time, but lately I've been wondering if the main thing that bonds us is our bodies. It's hardly surprising though: that's a pretty powerful bond when you're the only fat girls in your year. Who cares if you're different in pretty much every other way.

Before I muster the strength to pore through my piles of clothes, I check myself out. I do this on a semi-regular basis: stand in front of my full-length mirror and survey my body. Not looking for faults or flaws or things to get hung up on – just to look. I stand in a series of natural and unnatural poses, looking at my body from every angle so I can see it as other people see it. Standing in my perfectly high-waisted Marks and Spencer black knickers and my T-shirt bra, I see cute freckles over my face, light brown hair dangling to my chest that's gorgeous and thick (so I can tolerate the frizziness), pale blue eyes that don't even need accentuating with brown eyeshadow (like they tell you to do on YouTube – but that doesn't stop me anyway!), slightly overlapping front teeth . . . and fat.

There's a lot of fat.

Soft, pale thighs, squidgy tummy, deliciously squishy upper arms, round bum . . . not so much in the way of boobs . . . OK – enough posing. This outfit isn't going to choose itself.

I try on and discard various options: a sequinned top (too heavy for summer); my favourite casual-pretty sundress (needs wash). My denim cut-off shorts (seem like a good option if I'm going to engage in some light flirting but are maybe *too* short for a garden in Croydon rather than a summer holiday destination). I like the idea of a skirt and bare legs. I start rummaging in one of my 'to hang' piles for the skirt I had in mind when I hear the front door open and close (must be my mum, back from work), accompanied by the frenzied yelping of Ted the Yorkshire terrier, oily furball and rubbish guard dog extraordinaire. I quickly wriggle into my potential definite outfit when Mum appears at my bedroom door.

'What are you up to, sweet pea?' Mum asks, bangles jangling around her wrists as she pushes my door wide open. She hasn't knocked, as usual. Her belief that I'm not interesting enough to have anything to hide means she is pretty laissez-faire about personal space. At this point, I'm used to it.

'Nothing – just trying to decide what I'm going to wear to my friend's party tomorrow night,' I reply, as I finish pulling the skirt up to my waist.

Mum's eyes perceptibly widen in horror. 'You're thinking of wearing that? Don't you think it's a bit too clingy? Around your middle?'

'No! If I thought it looked bad, I wouldn't be wearing it, would I?'

'All I'm saying is, I wouldn't wear it.'

'Well you're not wearing it, are you?'

'I just want you to look nice! You have lots of outfits you look nice in, and this isn't one of them. This doesn't have to be a huge deal, Emily!'

'And all I want is to feel comfortable in what I'm wearing, and you seem to make it your sole purpose to make me feel uncomfortable about everything I like!' I snap.

'I just don't want people saying things about you – you know?'

'The only person who ever says anything bad is you!'

'Fine! I won't say a word about your clothes in future.'

She's lying.

'Good luck with that,' I mutter as she pads off to the kitchen.

My mum is totally beautiful, end of story. My sister and I pretty uniformly inherited our dad's less dramatic looks. Mum, though, is statuesque, with a pixie cut, big eyes and full lips. She's exactly the kind of person you would find yourself staring at if you saw them on the train or on the street or in the supermarket. There's something so magnetic about her, so enthralling. But none of this matters to her: if anyone does look at her, she thinks it's because she's fat. This fear governs her life and drives her to try anything to control it. If a diet exists, my mum will have tried it, guaranteed: grapefruit, Weight Watchers, cabbage soup, Slim Fast, master cleanse, South Beach, 5:2, paleo, blood type, Atkins, raw vegan, Slimming World, macrobiotic. She'll buy every exercise DVD going, and none makes it out of the cellophane. All her diets begin well; all end badly.

Me and my mum are fat for the same reason: food is delicious. So, any diet she tries is doomed to fail because it's depriving her of something she wants. You would have thought after three decades of dieting not working out for her, she would have taken the hint by now. But no – she's always chasing that impossible dream, always telling herself this time is different. It's never different.

I throw myself down on my bed in anger, letting out a roar of frustration. There is no one alive who can harsh my buzz quite like my mum. I want her to be on my team. I want her to be rooting for me. I realize that she's done more than just annoy me; she's set off a little prickle of fear in me. A little niggling doubt that asks, what if she's right? What if people do say things? No . . . I can't go down that route.

That's a slippery slope to grapefruits and a life of woe. I'm Emily Daly, and I literally do not worry about my body. I have never worried about my body and I don't plan to start now.

Somewhere under a pile of junk, my phone vibrates. As I dig it out from the heap of sequins, Lycra, lurex and wool, I see it's my sister. If someone's going to break the social contract and dare to ring me rather than message, I'm glad it's her.

'What's up, nerd,' I say in greeting as I lie back down on the bed.

'Hello, little one,' she replies. I can hear she's walking fast down a noisy street.

'How's la bella Manchester?'

'Bella as ever – not raining right now. I'm just walking to football practice.'

'How's the internship going? They must be releasing you back into the sweet embrace of uni soon, right?'

'Well, it's good, in that I'm doing a lot and I like the project I'm working on, but also quite rubbish because my boss is an A-plus creep. Today, he said he liked my perfume, then went on to lament the fact his wife never wears perfume, which he's decided means she never makes an effort for him – boo hoo, Martin. Way to put me off my nice floral Jo Malone.'

Katie is the queen from whom I learned the Art of Not Caring Too Much. She's very clever and good at everything she does. She's also super independent, only returning home briefly now and again from her hardworking life studying civil engineering in Manchester so my parents can feel like she still exists.

'Gross, gross, gross. Do you want me to beat him up for you?'

'No – I can't have my baby sister doing my dirty work for me. How are you, anyway? How are Mum and Dad?'

As I open my mouth to answer, I hear a high-pitched whistle like something from a cartoon, then Katie spitting out a gruff 'Jesus, I'd rather die'.

'Ooh – aren't you flavour of the month!'

'You would think my football kit would put them off, but the shorts seem to be sending the lads wild.'

'If it's giving you lots of pent-up anger to release at football, it's probably a good thing. Anyway . . . in answer to your question, I'm fine mostly, but just before you rang, old Helen was trying to have opinions on my wardrobe again,' I say.

Instantly I hear Katie sigh. 'Are you sure she was? Are you sure you're not just being sensitive?'

'No! God! She was literally telling me what not to wear because it shows the world I'm fat! That's exactly what just happened.'

'But she cares about you – she wouldn't want to upset you on purpose,' Katie says, clearly trying to placate me.

Not what I wanted to hear.

'Sorry, but you never get any of this from her. What makes you so sure that she wasn't trying to upset me? She thinks if she upsets me enough, I'll finally cave and eat nothing but salad for the rest of my life.'

It's amazing how quickly a conversation where Katie and I are on the same side can flip to one where we're adversaries. Katie has always been athletic, sporty, outdoorsy . . . and thin. Our colouring is the same, our hair the same frizzy thickness. We even have the same smattering of freckles, but our bodies are completely different. So of course she never had to listen to our mum telling her what not to wear, telling her how to make herself disappear, how to ensure she doesn't catch anyone's eye.

'OK, fine – you're right. But maybe you do wind her up a bit too. It's like you go out of your way to wear stuff you know she'll hate.'

'Nope! Nope, nope, nope. I'm not going to get into this with you. I'm not going to let this become my problem rather than her problem. I love my clothes. I love my style. And that's not my problem.' I feel overcome with a wave of bitterness. Of course Katie wouldn't understand. Of course I would have to defend myself like this.

'Maybe we shouldn't talk about this,' Katie says after going quiet for a moment.

'No! We! Shouldn't!' I say, putting the phone on speaker so I can clap between each word for emphasis, which I know annoys her.

I'm angry that she will never see my side of this. I feel betrayed. I hate arguing with Katie. Being four years apart in age means that we were close enough to be in the same house and the same school at the same time, but not so close that we were expected to come as a pair, to play together, to have things in common. And good job, because largely we don't. But we do usually get on well. That distance helped us avoid the screaming physical fights that my friends had with their siblings growing up. I could never steal her clothes when she lived here, for example. And we never wanted the same toys at the same time. So when we clash like this, it bothers me.

'I'm sorry, chicken. I love you. I'm nearly at football now,' she says in a soothing voice.

In the grand scheme of things, I'm still annoyed, but right now, I don't have the energy or the inclination to keep this skirmish going. She doesn't see our mum the way I do. She can't.

'I love you too, even though you're just *awful*,' I say, knowing she can hear the smile in my voice. 'And I hope you score a hat trick at football.'

'I'm the goalkeeper,' Katie says drily.

'Yeah, whatever,' I say, cackling down the phone. Pretending I don't know what Katie does when she's away is my favourite way to annoy her. 'Love you – bye!'

We hang up, and I stay flopped on my bed. Even though I've never wanted to be more like my sister, the way we look still finds a way to get its claws into our relationship. I've always known people see her as 'the pretty one', as if only one of us is allowed to be pretty, and by default it's Katie because she's thin. Then it's 'Emily with her great personality', as if Katie's a total bore. But that isn't what people mean. Katie could be the most accomplished, intelligent person in the room, and she would still be defined by the fact that she's good-looking. I could be the most boring person in the room (not that *that* would ever happen), and I would still be complimented on my personality rather than my looks. Our appearance, the way we both look on the surface, feels like such a stupid, unnecessary thing to worm its way into our minds, our relationship, our conversations – but there it is. We're capable of so much better, Katie and I.

We deserve so much better.

I channel Katie and decide not to escalate the situation with my mum over dinner. Also I can't be bothered to rehash it all in front of my dad, who will feel like he has to referee it. I notice Mum doesn't bring it up either.

After dinner, I deposit myself in the armchair and get started reading *Great Expectations* for next term's English classes, while my parents watch TV on the sofa. I'd only been planning to skim-read it with half an eye on whatever's on TV, but I find myself completely absorbed, and it's only when my dad announces that he's going to bed that I realize how late it is.

I'm about to say I'll do the same when my mum pipes up.

'Emily, do you want to . . . ?' she begins.

She doesn't need to say any more. I know what she's asking. My dad and my sister are early-to-bed, early-to-rise types, whereas my mum and I have always been night owls. The only time we really spend one-on-one is when we watch old films together when everyone else is asleep. It started when I was kind of young – too young to be staying up until midnight, anyway – but then it just became a question of Mum watching something, and me passively not going to bed, just sitting there and getting sucked into those technicolour worlds. And then over time, it evolved into our little thing – not every night, but sometimes.

Tonight, I'm tired and it's late, but I know that turning her down would be the wrong thing to do.

So I say yes, and while she's out in the kitchen making tea and retrieving two fondant fancies from the cupboard (literally my favourite food in the whole world), I hoist myself out of the armchair and move on to the sofa. And together we watch *Some Like It Hot*, not for the first time or even the second time, and I eat my pink fondant fancy off the little floral plate the way I always do: bite the icing off each side, scrape the fondant off the top with my teeth, and then eat the naked sponge on its own. My mum strokes my hair occasionally, and I don't bat her hand away like I sometimes want to, and we sit there — not perfect, but peaceful.

# CHAPTER THREE

'Fight for Your Right' – Beastie Boys

In the end, I decide to make a precisely medium amount of effort for Ben's party (black leather jacket over a slouchy Breton T-shirt and the offending jersey pencil skirt, accessorized with hoop earrings and red lipstick, naturally), and Abi, who always makes a more-than-medium amount of effort as a matter of principle, looks amazing. A tight dress and high platform sandals, and metallic gold eyeshadow on her lids, which stands out a mile against her dark skin and brings out the brown of her eyes.

Abi and I meet at the bus stop and make our way to Ben's house. Bottles clink gently in our bags as we head towards the source of a steady thumping noise. I take the screw-top bottle of white wine out of my bag and take a swig from it as we approach the door before offering it to Abi, who drinks daintily from it so as not to disturb her lip gloss.

'I was thinking about what you said,' I tell her in a business-like tone that I hope conceals my nervousness but think probably doesn't. I want Abi to know my goal for the evening. Saying it out loud means I'm duty-bound to carry it out.

'I say a lot of things,' says Abi archly.

'About getting stuff off the ground, about using tonight as an excuse to do a little flirting, make out with someone down the bottom of the garden, you know,' I say, wiggling my shoulders suggestively. 'Become a fully fledged Average Person.'

She squeals with delight. 'At last! This is the best news! You got this. I really believe in you. Thank you for giving me this excellent gift. Just go for it – what's the worst that can happen?'

Abi and I hang together for about five minutes at the party before the lure becomes just too great, and she gravitates towards Oliver, to whom she will be surgically attached for at least three hours. Ben, the epitome of hot masculinity, is doing pull-ups on a bar fixed over the living-room door, his afro brushing the ceiling. He and Kenji are taking it in turns to see who can do more in a row. Ella and Sophia are already gamely doing shots of something acid green with a group of girls from our year.

I drift in and out of conversations with a few people I vaguely know. I sip wine and I dance. And then I spy Ryan, and a smile creeps over my face. He has a warm sense of humour, a pretty good sense of style, thick, shiny, chocolate-brown hair, and he's always nice to me, even though we haven't spoken that much before. He's more than six feet tall with really broad shoulders and a kind puppy-dog face. He's good-looking, but in a sweet, harmless way. This makes perfect sense. Low risk, low emotional investment, potentially the perfect target. Bless you, Ryan Russell. Bless you.

I down the last of the wine from my plastic cup and try to saunter over as casually as possible. He's bent over the laptop that's controlling the music coming out of the speakers.

'You reckon some Run DMC?' he says.

'I reckon,' I reply, even though it's not true. I just don't want to bruise his ego so early in the night. It's not the moment for Run DMC – I know that. It's too late in the night, and people want pure pop bangers. But Ryan's in charge of the music, and I'm trying to get Ryan onside, not show him up with my sheer musical prowess.

'With great power comes great responsibility. My power is that people think my taste in music is good enough to sustain a party, which means I'm Playlist Master at every party.' He sighs with the apparent weight of his responsibility.

OK, so he's sort of right. His taste is Officially Good Enough To Sustain A Party, but his sense of timing is all off. I bet if they did a blind taste test of Ryan and me at the next party, I would emerge victorious as Playlist Master.

'Don't pretend you don't love it.' I smile, looking up at him through my heavily mascaraed lashes. It's part charm and part jealousy that it's not me in charge of the music.

He laughs. Of course he does. I'm charming him already.

'I do love it. I really love it. It gives me a sense of purpose, which can often be a major asset at parties. I can give good chat, but I never know how to seek the chat out, you know? Like how do you ever know the right time to slide into a conversation? How do you know when someone wants to talk to you? This is the kind of stuff I lie awake at night wondering about.'

I shrug. 'I think I just slide so freely into any and all conversations that I don't really worry about it. Hey, did you have a fun summer?'

'Yeah, I sure did. I hung out with the guys a bit. I've cycled my bike on every single road in the CR0 postcode, because why the hell not. I thrashed my brother on the PlayStation every day. So, all in all, a summer well spent. How about you?'

'I went away with my parents to Greece. I read about a hundred books. Paced every square inch of both the Whitgift and Centrale shopping centres. I feel like I should have done more with it, but not a lot I can do about that now,' I say.

We're getting on well, maintaining a flow back and forth.

This is a promising start! For someone I've only spoken to a few times before, we seem to have a pretty easy rapport. Maybe this was a good idea.

He takes a sip from his can and grimaces.

'What?' I ask.

'Tastes like piss,' he says.

'Did someone piss in it? Jesus, no one's that drunk, are they?'

'No, I think it was deliberately made this way. Do you think we're going to get used to how objectively disgusting alcohol tastes in time, or are all adults just pretending to enjoy it?' he says.

'My wine is mostly sugar, I think, and I'm pretty happy with that,' I say, looking at his lips as he takes another sip. I wonder how I'll know when the right moment has presented itself to make my move. Maybe I won't know. Oh no – that means I have to *make* it the right moment.

I watch him smile to himself as he cues up some tracks.

'Hey, do you want to go outside to . . .' I take a deep breath, deciding it's better if I take charge of the situation rather than waiting for it to appear. I lower my voice faux-suggestively. 'Get some *air*?'

As soon as I say it, I regret being so goofy, but thankfully the heavens have smiled on me, and he asks me to repeat myself because the music's too loud.

'What?' He looms closer to me so he can hear.

I should probably get the tone right this time. I mime fanning myself. 'It's kind of hot, huh? I'm going outside – do you want to come?'

Much better.

He cues another song before getting up, and we carry on talking as we head outside for some air.

The bench on the patio outside the sliding glass doors is empty, so we sit. This seems a good omen: outdoors equals romance, no? We're hardly alone though, as it's a warm night, and people have spilled outside on to the grass beyond the patio, smoking, chatting . . . but no one seems to be paying us any attention.

'So, are you still playing drums?' I ask, realizing I've retained at least a couple of pieces of information about Ryan over the time he's been on my radar.

'Yes, to my parents' distress. They regret the day they caved and bought me a drum kit,' he says with a grin.

'I remember seeing you in that joint concert we did. You were . . . really good. I can't imagine your parents have anything to complain about. It's not like you're sawing away at a violin or something,' I say.

'True. It's nice that you remember that,' he replies.

'Maybe I remember things about you . . . because I think you're cute.'

*What?!* I hadn't decided to say that at all. My mouth is running away from me, and I'm not sure how I feel about it. Maybe I've had too much wine. My stomach lurches with nerves as I wait to hear how he's going to take it. Maybe he'll pretend he didn't hear me . . .

Ryan's eyes widen, and he raises his eyebrows as if he's just registered what I said. He doesn't say anything. He straightens his back against the bench and breathes deeply. He still doesn't say anything. Then, against the odds, he turns his head towards me and looks at me for a few seconds. We're teetering on the precipice – it's surely only going in one direction. A weird little chant pops up in my brain going, *Kiss! Kiss! Kiss!*

This is so much easier than I thought it was going to be, and I cannot believe my luck. He smells sweet, with an alcoholic edge. His hair is ruffled, and his face looks relaxed, at ease. He moves in to pull me closer to him. As his hands make contact with the soft fat around my waist, he jolts back like he's been given an electric shock. No kiss. Yanked back from the precipice at the last moment. It's like the opposite of snatching victory from the jaws of defeat.

'This is a bad idea. I don't know what got into me. I'm really sorry. God, this is awkward,' he says, dropping his head into his hands, before looking up and surveying me. Surveying my body, to be precise. 'It's just . . . not right for me . . .' He trails off. He seems genuinely distressed at having to knock me back. Like that's meant to make me feel better.

It really doesn't.

'Look, Ryan, it's fine – whatever. Don't worry about it,' I say, exhaling so hard, it probably comes out as a snort. I'm burning with embarrassment, my face prickling with shame, but I try to laugh it off. Even though Ella had implanted this thought in my brain when she assumed that I'd want to lose weight to be romance ready, I'm still pretty taken aback to discover my body is the number one turn-off for someone who might otherwise be interested in me.

Ryan mumbles something about needing to return to his DJing, gets up, and stalks back into the house, shaking his head. Mostly at himself, I reckon – but it feels like it's at me too.

'What are you doing out here all on your own?'

Sophia's head has appeared from round the patio doors like a cartoon character. She is absolutely not going to tolerate me avoiding the party, so she drags me back inside. Dancing to 90s R & B with Ella and Sophia is obviously the cure to all my problems. But as we dance, I feel myself zoning out, retreating into my thoughts while my body moves on its own.

What even happened? I'm cute . . . Ryan's cute . . . Maybe

I'm not wild about him, but did I have to be? I didn't think so. Maybe he's not wild about me either, but at least he liked me. I'm sure I didn't get that wrong, but the second he was faced with the actual reality of my body, he flipped out. Have I been kidding myself all this time? What. The. Hell? I thought it was going to be simple: I decide to make a bit of an effort, flutter my eyelashes a bit, do fewer weird jokes, do more actual flirting, and BAM! It would prove a recipe for success. Turns out my stupid body is going to get in the way. I thought Ryan was cool. I mean, he wasn't the love of my life, but I thought he was cute enough to kiss at least once . . .

Emily: Officially Too Fat for Kissing.

Just after midnight, I take a break from dancing, and Abi takes a break from making out with Oliver. We find ourselves together on the patio bench, quietly eyeing the boys further down the lawn, who are gently swaying after a few drinks.

'Oh my GOD – how did your plan work out?' Abi asks, suddenly animated.

'Disastrously,' I say. I figure there's no point lying. 'I thought Ryan was a good idea.'

'Yes, he totally is. Why have I never thought of this before?!' she says, but then my words catch up with her. 'Wait – why?'

'Disaster because he seemed like he was going to go for it and then at the last minute freaked out. As soon as he touched me, he freaked out. My body freaked him out.'

She looks awkward, like she doesn't know what to say. 'Damn, I'm sorry . . . I mean, I'm sure it wasn't that. I'm sure it wasn't about your body. I'm sure it was something else . . .' She trails off. 'I'm sure he didn't do it on purpose.'

'No, I'm sure he didn't,' I say, placing a hand on hers and squeezing it reassuringly. Even though I'm the one who needs reassurance. Of course she wouldn't understand. But I'm not in the mood to explain the fact that it definitely was about my body. I sigh. 'I wasn't even that into him. I can't tell if that makes it better or worse.'

All of a sudden, I decide I've had enough for tonight. I get up off the bench, say bye to Abi, and head into the house, up the stairs, and into the bedroom where I dumped my jacket earlier. I can barely summon the energy to move my arms as I rummage through the pile of jackets and sweaters searching for mine. I'm lost in my thoughts as I head back downstairs, hoping to slip away without bumping into Ryan again, when I spot something familiar: the cover of the album *Talking Heads: 77* on someone's T-shirt. Clearly this is someone I need to know. My eyes travel up from the T-shirt to its owner's face. I feel an electric charge pass through the air around me as I make eye contact with . . .

Who . . . ? Who the hell is that?

Disclaimer: I have never actually been shot. I would imagine, though, that it feels quite a lot like the way I feel when I see him for the first time. I keep walking down the stairs, my heart in my throat and racing a million miles an hour. Don't trip on the stairs . . . One foot in front of the other . . . You've got this . . . You remember how to walk.

I exhale deeply as I cross the crowded room to the door, and as I breathe out, it's as if my body is breathing out an '*Oh my God*' and breathing in a new energy – a changed thing. The door . . . You're walking to the door. The door that the guy is standing near. I've never seen him before in my life. I would remember if I had. Jesus – I would remember. Has he been here the whole night? How did I miss him until now? I wonder if we were just moving around the party in different directions the whole time.

What do I do? Am I just meant to leave without knowing anything about him? Without even knowing his name? I have seconds to decide. Maybe I should talk to him? But what would I say? I'll think of something.

And then I remember Ryan's touch, the way he shrank away from me, and all my confidence shrinks away too. The fire of optimism doused with the freezing cold water of rejection. I feel like I physically shudder, though I'm pretty sure I don't.

It's resolved: I'm leaving.

Before I make it through the front door, I bump into Ella, who's indignant that I would even consider making an exit without saying goodbye. It's hard to get out of a party anyway, and all the time I'm trying to switch off my hyper-awareness of where this mystery guy is in the room. I don't want to know where he is or what he's doing or who he's talking to. If I see him again, I'll never stop looking.

Finally, Ella lets me leave. And I've managed to avoid seeing him. I push the door open and head out into the dark, cool night, lifting my head to the sky to take in the stars. Almost instantly I'm brought back down to earth as my foot makes contact with something solid on the step in front of me, making me stumble and swear. Everyone's smoking in the back garden, so why the hell is some idiot sitting smoking on the front steps, precisely where they might get kicked by people leaving—

Oh no. It's him.

'Woah! Sorry – it's a bad place to sit, isn't it,' he says as he scrambles to his feet, hastily stubbing his cigarette out.

I can't think of anything clever or witty or sexy to say. Quick, think of something – anything – just make it alluring, enticing and sophisticated.

'Yeah, it is a bit,' I reply. Good one, Emily, mate. I'm

glad it's dark; I don't think I could take being this close to him, being able to see him right in front of me.

He checks me over. 'You didn't hurt yourself, did you?'

'Fortunately for you, there will be no lawsuit,' I reply. Even in the dark, I can see his gorgeous smile.

'That's a relief. Well, I won't keep you,' he says.

Keep me, I think. Please keep me.

'Yeah. Um, bye, I guess,' I say, making everything unnecessarily awkward as I turn to walk down the drive. My steps trigger a security light, the glow gently illuminating the porch. I do the one thing I didn't want to do: I turn back to look at him. I try to take all of him in at once, try to memorize the parts that I can make out in the low light. He's tall, kind of solid-looking. He stands straight. His hair is messy, a dirty golden blond, and he keeps running his hands through it. Big, clear, bright blue eyes behind glasses. Full lips. No, improbably full lips, which are completely beautiful, and which I totally want to kiss right this second. Kind of flushed cheeks. He looks soft and warm, a gentle place to be. I want to be there—

'I'm Joe, by the way,' he says, breaking my reverie. 'Nice to meet you.'

'I'm Emily. And yes, I guess it was.' I smile at him. 'Hey . . .' I add uncertainly, 'I like your T-shirt.'

He looks down at himself, like he can't quite work out

why someone might say that to him, realizes he's wearing a Talking Heads T-shirt and grins. 'Oh, cheers! You . . . like them? Or you just like green writing on a red background?'

'No – I like them. A lot. Maybe I would go as far as to say they're my favourite band.'

'They're something more than cool. He's the coolest.'

I have nothing to say to that except, 'Yes.' I shrug nonchalantly, although my heart is fluttering, and my head is spinning.

'Glad we're in agreement,' he says, flashing me another smile that makes me feel weak. His teeth are straight and white and perfect. Of course they are.

'Well, it was cool to meet you,' I say, as I start back down the drive.

'Yeah, nice to meet you, Emily.'

I meander home, all the way along the endless main road that leads from South Croydon straight to the bottom of my road in Purley. I need time to process the electric crackle that I felt inside my chest, the fizz that has just completely short-circuited me. As I wait for a set of traffic lights to change on Croydon Road, I try to assess what I know about this guy. His name is Joe. He likes Talking Heads. He's kind of charming. He is, to use the technical term, *well fit*. The fact he's well fit is certainly sweetening the deal, but . . . I just know that this isn't all there is to it. We have something in common. And if we have one something in common (and music is an important something to me), maybe we have more somethings in common.

I have had crushes before: my neighbour; a boy from another school who was always on my bus in the morning; our Year Nine maths teacher. I mean, I *thought* I'd had crushes before. So why do I feel like I've been hit by a truck? Minutes earlier, I had no idea this boy even existed, and now I feel like I will surely die if I don't know everything about him, touch every part of his body, consume his soul, and make him love me for the rest of my life. Based on what? Based on nothing. Is this what people mean when they talk about chemistry? Can chemistry be one-sided? Is this what love at first sight feels like?

I feel dazed and light-headed, but at the same time, like all my senses have been turned on at once, like all the blood is rushing towards my heart, like I'm going to be lifted out of my shoes. It's as if someone has put a spell on me, and I'm no longer under my own control. My body is prickling, my brain whirring at lightning speed. I don't know what's going on, but I know everything has changed. I have a purpose. I have a goal: get to know that guy.

Before I know it, I've carried myself home. At the bottom of our drive, I hop from one foot to another and screw my face up in a silent scream, trying to get some of the pent-up energy out of my system in case one of my parents is still awake and wants to engage me in conversation. The energy flowing out of me is a mixture of lust for this Joe, whoever he is, and crushing despair at how much more difficult the whole thing is going to be because of . . . well . . . this *body* that I'm currently shaking out on the pavement outside my house.

Bodies. Who needs them?

# CHAPTER FOUR

### 'Something Changed' – Pulp

Rise and shine, Emily Daly! Today is the first day of the rest of your life, and you are in love!

So far, being in love mostly blows. I feel on edge and stressed and faintly nauseous. I'm giving *Being in Love* a one-star review. I'm loitering in my bed post-party until it's absolutely necessary to face the world (the world that my crush lives in), and my productivity can just about stretch to scrolling through the music library on my phone and compiling a playlist to match my mood. Curating a tracklist to encapsulate the highs and lows of feeling like this:

'I Want the One I Can't Have' – the Smiths
'What Have I Done to Deserve This' – Pet Shop Boys
'How Will I Know' – Whitney Houston
'Fantasy' – Mariah Carey
'Something Changed' – Pulp

Before I can locate the perfect follow-up to Jarvis Cocker's impassioned crooning, there's a knock on my door. This means it's my dad, since, unlike my mum, he was blessed with respect for personal space.

'Emily?'

'You can come in,' I call back, and my dad sheepishly pushes the door open.

'Did you have a nice time at the party last night, treasure?' he asks, sitting down on my bed.

'Yeah, it was OK. It was fun,' I reply, not knowing what to say.

How do I fully communicate the utterly grim misery of being rejected by someone I didn't even fancy that much because I'm fat, then meeting the person I now fancy the most in the whole world, who I probably don't stand a chance with because, oh look, I'm still fat.

'Are you all right? You seem a bit . . . subdued. Did you have too much to drink?' He winks slyly at me, the skin around his kind brown eyes crinkling behind his glasses. I think my dad wishes I was more rebellious, had more fun, was more creative, artistic, bohemian, whatever.

'No, Dad – I didn't. And even if I did, I wouldn't tell you.'

'You can tell me anything, pet,' he says.

And it breaks my heart because I know it's true, but at the same time, it's not true at all. Just because he would be ready to hear anything, it doesn't mean I'm always ready to tell him anything. Like when I was bullied at primary school, I could never, ever bring myself to tell him or my mum because I knew they would worry, and I didn't want to do that to them. So odds are, I'm probably not about to open the floodgates and launch into an impassioned word-vomit about being gripped by a sudden obsessive fear that no one will ever want me because I'm fat . . . all before breakfast.

'I know,' I mumble instead, feeling guilty. 'Thank you. Anyway, what did you want?'

'I'm going to take Ted for a walk. Do you want to come?'

Ordinarily I would say no, because hibernation is my default state, but I'm experiencing a rush of good feeling towards my dad and don't want to turn him down. Plus, I've been a bad dog owner recently and haven't paid much attention to Ted, so maybe now I can bond with both of them. I throw back the covers and get out of bed, slip on some jogging bottoms and my dad's old Pixies T-shirt (I may like good clothes, but even I know that not all expeditions require them), and twist my hair into an ugly top knot. I'm almost ready to hit the streets. The not-at-all-mean streets of suburban Purley, more specifically.

I pad downstairs in search of trainers and find my mum sitting at the kitchen table with her back to me, tapping away on her laptop. The way she whips around when she hears my footsteps alerts me to the distinct possibility she's up to something dubious. I crane my neck to see what's on her screen, and just before she has a chance to hit the X and close the window, I spot the words 'Wellness System'. Dubious indeed.

'Are you going out with Dad?' she says breezily, as if she's got nothing to hide.

'Uh, yeah. Are you coming?' I'll play along. I don't care what she's looking at (except I clearly do).

'No, I'm just going to stay here,' she says, smiling weakly.

'OK.'

I turn away and busy myself with finding Ted's lead, but while I'm rummaging in the cupboard, I take out my phone and search for 'Wellness System'. To the surprise of absolutely no one, it turns out to be a new diet concept. Here we go again.

As the front door slams behind us, I wonder if I should bring what is clearly Mum's latest diet fad up with my dad, but I decide not to. I have nothing new to say about her obsession with dieting. I'm tired of hearing about diets, tired of talking about diets, tired of feeling like she's scrutinizing and evaluating my body every time she looks at me.

It's the perfect kind of day, with a pale sun in a blue sky and a cool breeze on the trees. For once, I'm glad to be outside. We stroll up and down the streets of our neighbourhood, chatting about my sister and how she's doing in Manchester, trading opinions on the new album by John Grant before concluding we both like it. It hits me how well I get on with Dad, not least in comparison to the non-stop tension I have with my mum. I'm grateful; some people don't even have a peaceful relationship with one parent.

I'm doing well keeping up with the conversation, but in my head, my thoughts keep tuning in and out to Joe. What's Joe doing right now? Where does he live? What's his story? What's he thinking about right now (because it sure as hell won't be me)? . . . I'm glad he can't see me at this very moment because I probably look like a rubbish bag full of soil. But I'd like to be able to see him, just to keep an eye on him, see what he's up to. Normal stuff. What I'm saying is I want to go full creep and install CCTV in his home, I guess.

After we decide that Ted has stretched his tiny legs long enough, my dad, aka Masterchef, remembers he needs to buy capers to give lunch that certain sharp, salty *je ne sais quoi*. A trip to Big Tesco is in order on the way home. Now, there is truly nothing I love more in this world than a huge supermarket. A supermarket on two levels with a slow-moving travelator and rotisserie chickens is my idea of a good time, so I'm not complaining. Except, of course, I have to stay outside with Ted because I can't be trusted to choose the right kind of capers. So, I'm holding him in my arms and rocking him like a baby when I hear someone shout my name. Musical, slightly accented: 'Emily!'

At first, I can't locate the source of the voice, but after a few slow-mo seconds spinning around looking for who has spoken my name, I lock eyes with . . . No! It can't be. But . . . it *is*. Camila! Thank God she's back! Except as I take her in, it doesn't really look like her at all. As I'm trying to process what I'm seeing, her mum, who's busy loading bags into the boot of their car, waves to me, and Camila jogs over, beaming, and throws her arms around me. There's a lot less of her for me to hug back.

To my adoring mind, Camila has always been the most beautiful angel to grace the planet. The Chilean genes on her mum's side give her thick, heavy, straight dark hair, and the Swedish on her dad's give her a wide, open face. Except, today, her hair is lighter, bleached with ashy highlights throughout, and her wide face appears less fleshy. She's also wearing make-up, when in all the years I've known her, she's shown no interest in it. I've always been the one into clothes and beauty, while Camila stuck to a pretty standard uniform of neutral basics, trying to draw as little attention to herself as possible. Because Camila, unlike me, has always thought there is something wrong with being fat. And now, after only a couple of months in Sweden, she's melted some of it away. Not loads, but . . . some. Enough to make a noticeable difference. And along with the make-up, the hair, the clothes, it all adds up to a totally different picture.

It's been just eight weeks – how could she possibly look so different? It's like she's been on a weird makeover show, or like she's been on several different weird makeover shows at once, where they've tackled every element of what it means to be Camila. Or, I guess, what it means to *look* like Camila. Was she abducted and brainwashed in Sweden?

'Well, you look . . . different,' I say, deadpan. Even though I'm reeling, a more calculating part of my brain is already assessing the implications of this for me – namely that I'm now, officially, the only fat one in my year at school.

'Yeah, I guess so,' she says, sounding sort of obtuse.

I have no problem saying she looks really nice. Her make-up suits her; it brings out her eyes. It's not like she couldn't wear make-up before. It's just that she never did. And she's traded in her jeans and hoody for a folksy-patterned smock dress with ankle boots. Also good choices. I'm already wondering if she thought there was simply no point bothering while she was fatter.

'So . . . how? What? Why?'

'Um, to be honest, when I got to my grandma's, I remembered how relentless my cousins are to me about my body, and something just snapped. I basically got bullied into changing the way I look,' she says, shrugging.

Brainwashed in Sweden wasn't far wrong.

'I always hated your cousins,' I say. I can't help myself. It's one thing if Camila wants to change the way she looks, but if her horrible rich cousins are going to be the ones to force her into it, then I'm not going to pretend that's legit. But obviously it's the wrong thing to say because she instantly goes on the defensive, despite the fact she's said about a million times how awful they are. I guess she's sort of transferred over to their side now.

'Actually, they're pretty cool. Anyway, they were only ever mean to me for my own good. I saw them a lot this summer, and I really think you'd like them if you got to know them,' she says earnestly.

I doubt it. 'OK, whatever. So, what did you do – work out for, like, ten hours every day?'

'No. I swam a lot and did some walking. To be honest, it was the fact my grandparents were there that meant I finally caved. My gran was always in on the plot to get me to look more like the Swedish side of my family, so she leaped at the chance to starve her granddaughter for the summer. I basically couldn't eat unless my grandparents fed me, and they knew I was already sort of . . . trying to eat less.'

'What about the whole . . .' I gesture vaguely with my hand in the direction of her head.

'Oh, you mean the make-up and the hair stuff? My cousin Linnea took me into Stockholm shopping one Saturday, and we went to the salon she goes to. It looks better, right?'

'I liked it black. It was cool. It was you. But this looks nice too,' I say pathetically. Maybe I don't like change in other people. I wonder if her Chilean grandparents, settled in another part of Sweden, had seen her, and what they thought of this dramatic transformation.

I thought the first thing I would do upon being reunited with Camila at school tomorrow would be to sit down together and catch up on her summer away, bond over some awfulness her cousins perpetrated, before briefing her on the fact that I'm one hundred per cent definitely in love with a guy I've only just met. But this unexpected meeting has really thrown me off.

Camila glances towards the car park. 'My mum's waiting – I'd better go. I'll see you in the morning anyway, right?'

'Right,' I say.

We hug. I can already feel that it's not the same.

Right on cue, my dad emerges from Tesco.

'Who were you talking to?' he asks, taking Ted's lead from me as we start our walk home.

I don't fancy explaining my woes to him right now.

'Camila,' I reply, as naturally as possible.

'Camila? Like, your friend Camila? Camila Forsberg?' He even has the skill and politeness to pronounce her name properly, something hardly anyone English does.

'The one and only.'

I feel deflated. I hate that this has hit me so hard, but I really did love having a comrade. And right now, I need a comrade more than ever, given that I'm attempting to fling myself on to the wild battlefield of romance. Camila used to be slow and unbothered about boys too. It didn't matter that no one ever fancied either of us. We could just hang out together at parties, not trying to seduce anyone. All of a sudden, I feel like she's probably some kind of skilled foxy temptress.

'It didn't look like her . . .' My dad looks back over his shoulder, trying to get another glimpse at Camila, but she's long gone.

'No, it didn't, did it,' I say.

Dad knows better than to push it. Instead he tells me the idea he's had for a new play, but I'm not really listening, and I feel bad about that. But there's just too much swirling around in my head. I play and replay the conversation with Camila. There was weird, prickly tension. I know I'm not just imagining it. But of course there would be; of course it would be awkward; of course we'd need some time to warm up. We haven't seen each other for a couple of months. I couldn't even Skype her on the Island of No Internet. And of course there's the dramatic image overhaul. But I can't pretend I shouldn't have been kinder to her, however wounded I felt. Maybe I went a bit hard.

Can I even be sure of anything any more? Up is down! Black is white! Animals are walking on their heads! Being in love is actually terrible! I almost didn't recognize my best friend!

I'm well aware it makes me a rubbish person, but sometimes you can't help but see things through the lens of *'But what does this mean for me?'* No, Emily – it's not always about you. But sometimes it sure does feel like it. Only a couple of days ago, I was trundling along nicely, and now everything's turned on its head – just in time for going back to school in the morning. I always felt like I had loads of time stretching out ahead of me and endless opportunities to do things over again and get them right, but this time is the last time. One more year of school and then that's it: the real world.

Later, after an afternoon bath (a bath always feels like the right thing to do before a big day), I dig out last year's pencil case and shove it in my school bag. True preparation! I sink into the sofa and am about settle down to watch the omnibus of a reality-TV show involving inept grooms choosing their brides' wedding dresses when my phone vibrates with a message.

Camila

So weird running into you earlier!
Do you want to hang this evening?

Do I? I mean, I would never normally think twice about it.

Yeah, go on.

I'll have to get used to New Camila sooner or later, so I agree to go over to hers after dinner for a bit. It's easy as she lives so close, and I can walk it, so once I've eaten with my parents, I disappear off to Camila's.

On the way there, I think about Joe, because it's a nice place for my mind to wander when I don't have to think about anything else. Maybe I need to ration myself – like only thinking about Joe three times a day. Maybe four. He's just so cute, though – what else am I meant to think about?

When I press the doorbell at Camila's house, she's at the door within seconds and pulls me into a tight hug. She makes the soft cooing noise of a wood pigeon in my ear, and I make it back – a weird greeting ritual we started in our first year at secondary school when we had our lessons in a damp Portakabin with incredibly loud pigeons nesting in the roof. I guess some things never change.

Her parents yell hellos at me as we dash upstairs to her room where we can recline on huge beanbags in peace and play loud music. Camila doesn't even like loud music; she just turns it up for my benefit when I come over.

Camila sighs. 'I'm so bummed I missed Ben's party last night. I didn't get home till really late from the airport.' She takes a sip of her orange juice through a bendy straw.

'You didn't miss much . . .' I say, not sure if I want to let my crush out into the world. Or talk about the weird non-kiss with Ryan. Especially now Camila is looking so . . . un-Camila. It would make me feel exposed, going into all the bad feelings that got stirred up when he reacted to my body the way he did, and now doesn't feel like the right time.

'Really? Nothing to report?'

I twist my hair around my finger, going cross-eyed as I hunt for split ends, trying to make up my mind if I should tell Camila about Joe. 'Well –' my mouth can't hold it in any longer – 'there was one thing. I met this guy as I was leaving the party, and I'm, like, basically obsessed with him now.'

'Oh my God! What? That's not your usual style at all.'

She knows me too well, clearly.

'Yeah, I know . . . It's all very new and extremely horrible.'

'Why horrible?' Camila drains the last of the orange juice with a hoarse sucking noise as it travels up the straw.

'I don't know, man. It just feels so embarrassing. Having feelings. Exposing yourself to rejection and other terrible things.'

'No! You've got to be optimistic! Then good things will happen. You're just asking for trouble when you go into it with a neg attitude,' she says emphatically.

This isn't new, by the way – she's always been a big believer in the innate goodness and romance of the world.

'I'm just being realistic,' I say with a huff.

'Tell me about him though.'

'I literally don't know anything other than his name is Joe, and he's nauseatingly cute. It was just a feeling, you know? Like a connection.'

'I don't know, but I'll take your word for it.'

Camila and I have always been in the same boat: just a bit cut off from romance. I wonder if that'll change now. I'm still finding it weird just *looking* at her. Taking in how different she looks, not just compared to herself at the end of last term, but compared to me too.

'I feel like when I know, I'll know,' she adds.

'That's the thing – you're actually waiting for . . . the One, or whatever you want to call it. Whereas I just haven't been bothered until now. And I hate being bothered, as you know.'

Camila smiles. 'A disruption to normal service.'

'Yep. I just like things floating along nicely, the occasional bright spot on the horizon to look forward to, but otherwise I don't want stuff interrupting my flow. And this is an interruption of epic proportions.'

She nudges me with a shoulder. 'But you have no idea how this will play out. Maybe he's going to be the love of your life.'

'Or more likely I'll spend a week thinking about him then never see him again and forget about him by half-term,' I say, and I half hope it's true. 'There was this other thing . . .' I begin, before I can help myself.

'What other thing?'

I think for a moment and then decide I don't want to share Ryan's brush-off and my internal fat-shame flare-up with Camila. Dealing with uncomfortable emotions has never been my strong suit. 'Oh, nothing,' I say instead. 'It's too boring to tell.'

We waste the rest of the evening watching back-to-back episodes of *Keeping Up with the Kardashians* that Camila recorded on Series Link while she was away. Neither of us talks any more about her new body, but when I walk home that night, I feel a little cloud of loneliness settle around me: I'm the last one standing.

# CHAPTER FIVE

'Close to Me' – The Cure

The first thing I hear when I open the door to our form room is the one thing I could really do without hearing.

'Oh my God, Camila – you look amazing!' Holly squeals, stretching out all the vowels.

I thought maybe I could hide from weight chat at school, even if I can't avoid it at home. But no – that's obviously too much to ask for. Now, Holly. Horrible Holly. The word 'frenemy' was invented for Holly. She's kind of cool, kind of evil. You wish she would just be your friend, but she insists on existing behind this fence of barbed wire where no one can get too close. Being nice to her just makes you feel pathetic because you know you're only doing it as insurance against future meanness, but actually being mean to her doesn't really come naturally to me. It's easier to maintain a cordial distance. You wish she would just chill the hell out. Anyway, right now she's praising my best friend for reappearing after the summer holidays several pounds lighter.

'Emily, don't you think Camila looks amazing?'

Not even a hello, and she knows she's doing it. She has a wolfish glint in her eye.

'Like, really amazing.'

'Oh sure – Camila always looks amazing,' I say, trying to keep the prickle out of my voice as I dump my bag on the desk.

'Thanks, girl,' Camila says, coming over to hug me, doing her best to deflect Holly's stirring.

Holly is smiling to herself. It's as if within seconds, she's assessed the change in dynamic between Camila and me. We're no longer the Fat Emily and Fat Camila duo – I'm now definitely the odd one out. I'm sure Holly loves it.

As I discover throughout the day, Camila's change in shape is the hot topic of conversation. When we go out at lunchtime to get a sandwich, a boy on his break at the supermarket eyes her appreciatively. When we sit down in English class, Mrs Mackinnon does a double take. I grit my teeth through various versions of the same back and forth that played out with Holly earlier. Who knew other people's weight could be so interesting to so many? It's poking a little hole in me, scratching away at the place that says, *'People are so obsessed with the way you look.'*

Although she started the day glowing with pride, Camila seems bored of talking about it now, for the most part anyway. And I'm *definitely* bored of talking about it. But it's not all bad being back at school: my timetable is sweet, and Camila, Abi, Ella, Sophia and I all have the same free period on a Monday afternoon. We can lounge about in the common room, and one hundred per cent definitely not spend it doing coursework. It could be a lot worse.

Today, we're sprawled on an array of soft, low chairs by the window, taking it in turns to flick through a copy of a women's magazine that Priyanka threw at us before dashing off to biology. It's pretty rubbish, to put it plainly – just full of clothes for people who are extremely rich and extremely thin, celebrity interviews where they reveal nothing, and – oh look – some perilous-looking diet.

'Ugh!' I burst out, tossing the magazine to Abi. 'And this agony aunt is a literal idiot – she's given such bad advice, the person that wrote in should actually sue her.'

'Why?' Ella asks. 'What did she say?'

Abi clears her throat, preparing to read. 'OK, so the reader asked, "How do I communicate in bed without having a panic attack? I find it so hard to articulate what I'm feeling and what I want, and I find I can't make the words come out without sending myself into this huge spiral of anxiety that's kind of a downer on sex. I really need your help!"'

'A fair question,' says Camila.

'Yeah, but the answer was just like . . . "You don't have

to communicate with words. Use your body language!" Which feels like kind of an irresponsible answer, right?'

'What do you mean?' Sophia raises a sceptical eyebrow.

'OK, so first things first. I know I have, like, zero experience in this area,' I say, rolling my eyes. 'But, general principles apply! Obviously the big problem is that, like . . . people don't want to talk about sex because they're embarrassed or something, but also it feels like we're bad at setting boundaries in general. Like, it's not just a problem that starts with sex – it's a problem that starts way, way back in other parts of our lives. We force ourselves to do things we don't want to do in general, and then we're expected to be able to give firm "yes" and "no" answers when it comes to sex! It's wild. Anyway – telling someone to communicate about what they want or don't want in bed using body language seems like a bad idea. Like, shouldn't we be trying to get people to talk more rather than less?'

The group silently absorbs my rant for a second.

'But what do you think the woman who asked the question should do instead?' Camila says.

'Uhhh . . .' I think for a moment. 'I don't think I'd wait until I was naked in bed with someone, about to have sex with them, to say what I do or don't want. Like, waiting until you're about to have sex to talk about sex feels like a lot of pressure – like, it might sound personal . . . or

58

come across as a criticism of your partner. Also, if you chat about it in a non-sexy scenario instead, it's not like you'd have to put everything into practice straight away – it's just like a helpful little FYI for next time. That would be my advice: keep your clothes on; keep the pressure off. Everyone wins.'

'But how? Talking is so . . . awkward,' Camila says.

'Look, I don't actually know, but I would bring it up casually, like something you want to talk about to make it better for both of you. Spin it as an opportunity for your partner to enjoy sex more because you'll enjoy it more. I guess make it a fun conversation about what you're into or what you're curious about or what you're really not into, if that's the thing you need to bring up.'

We all sit in silence for a second.

'Here endeth my thoughts.'

'You're so wise,' Abi says, sighing. 'Everything you say makes me feel better about everything. Less scared.'

'Don't you think that sounds kind of . . . stressful, though?' asks Camila, chewing her lip.

'What's stressful?' says Abi.

'Saying stuff like, "This is what I want to do; this is what I don't want to do" to someone you're sleeping with.'

Abi shrugs. 'Maybe the first time you say it, because being honest is hard, and talking about what you want is hard. But I would rather get what I want than hope they can just figure it out with no direction.'

'Honestly, giving advice about having hypothetical sex is stressful enough, never mind thinking about actual real-life sex one day. It's all too much, guys,' I say, rummaging in my bag for my timetable. At least I feel comfortable with my friends knowing that I'm most definitely and certifiably A Virgin.

'Good job there's literally no chance of it happening then, eh?'

We all turn our heads to Holly, who's making a cup of tea at the sink while doing a healthy dose of eavesdropping. Holly doesn't take her eyes off her phone to look at us, just keeps scrolling away absent-mindedly with a smug smile on her face.

'Get out of here, Holly,' Abi spits back at her.

'Chill, Abi – it was only a joke,' says Holly, rolling her eyes.

It was definitely *not* a joke. First, because it's true. And second, because she knows she only said it to make me feel bad.

'Is there not a single living soul that you're interested in? Still?' asks Ella, totally incredulous.

Now seems like as good an opportunity as ever to fess up about Joe. Introduce the concept to the world. Come out as a crush-haver.

'Actually . . .' I say, and even with just that word, I can't help smiling. I've got a secret. A little something no one knows but me. But not for long.

'Oh my God, what the hell?' cries Ella. 'What's going on?!'

Everyone leans in.

'Jesus, it's not that exciting; it's definitely not a . . . thing. I just met someone the other day that I thought was quite cute,' I say, in what may be the understatement of the century. I've thought about him non-stop for two days. I've thought about his face, his hands, his voice, the colour of his hair, the jeans he was wearing. But the gnawing doubt that guys like him don't go for girls like me has also filled my head. I'm embarrassed even to think like this, and I feel exposed and vulnerable.

'Who, though?' Abi looks at me seriously. 'We need a name . . . a star sign.'

'Um, just this guy I met at Ben's party. So, no star sign just yet,' I say, tugging at my top, not looking anyone in the eye. 'I didn't really talk to him much, but I thought he was pretty OK-looking . . .' There I go again with the understatements. At least Camila doesn't blow my cover and let on we've already discussed this in private.

'We still need a name,' says Abi, clearly thirsty for details.

'Joe. His name is Joe,' I say, like I'd been nervously holding my breath. Saying his name out loud makes it real. Multiple human people knowing I fancy him makes it . . . a thing. It's not just a thing rattling around in my head or a secret shared with my best friend. It's a real thing that I might just have to deal with.

Sophia leans forward. 'What does he look like? Is he cute?'

'I think so! He's taller than me, blond hair, kind of . . . normal size? God, I don't know how to describe him! He has really nice lips though.'

Abi cocks her head. 'Waaaaaait a minute, my girl. If he's the boy I'm thinking of, I literally just saw him.'

'Saw him where? What do you mean?' I'm starting to panic – this is too real already. I thought he only really existed in my head, in my own little world. It hadn't occurred to me that he is an actual person who is walking around, breathing, talking to people, eating food, being places.

'When I went out at lunch to see Oliver for a bit, we went down a . . . secluded, romantic side street to make out,' she says, waggling her eyebrows. 'And he bumped into someone he knew going into a shop there, and then after the guy had gone, Oliver said that it was Joe who had been at Ben's party the other night – as if I'm going to remember everyone I meet when I'm drunk! Anyway, he works in that record shop, the weird second-hand one round the corner. Apparently his family runs it or something.'

'What did he look like? Lemme just check this is actually the same guy,' I say breathlessly.

'Um . . . kind of exactly how you just said, but also he was wearing some sort of band T-shirt that would probably appeal to you.'

'That's the one . . .'

Woah! Way too much information, way too quickly. Too real. Yep, I definitely liked it better when he could be written off as a figment of my imagination. So now I know where Joe is right at this very minute. Why is this so . . . weirdly stressful? Why does it matter where he is? I think about it for a second and realize it's because now I know where he is, I feel like I need to be there. Like, now.

Ella nudges me. 'You should go and see him. This is perfect.'

She's totally right, encouraging me to do what I was desperately hoping no one would encourage me to do. Knots gnaw away in the pit of my stomach while a wild fluttering starts in my chest.

'Maybe . . .' I mumble, but they're all buoyed by my newfound crush and the news that he's mere streets away from us. How can they think this is exciting and fun? Do they not realize it's actually extremely bad and stressful—

I'm literally saved by the bell: break-time's over, and to my friends' great disappointment, we have to head off to our next classes. No more time for gossip.

I daydream all the way through physics with Mrs Shah. I can't stop zoning out, even though I desperately need to tune in. Let me assure you: physics is no joke. Never has been, never will be. When the double lesson finishes, I realize I've written hardly any notes. I've spent the whole class burrowed deep inside my own head, playing out various scenarios where I visit the shop where Joe works after school.

Oh God, creep mode fully engaged.

# CHAPTER SIX

'This Must Be the Place' – Talking Heads

'I don't want to look like a weirdo. That's literally the last thing I want to look like,' I whine at Abi and Camila.

'You won't!' Camila says, an imploring look in her eyes.

She's being extremely optimistic.

We're sitting on a bench outside school. It's 3.45 p.m., and the clock is most definitely ticking.

'This is your chance, mate! It's not weird for you to just . . . drop by while he's at work,' says Abi.

I shoot her a look so she understands that some things will always seem creepy, and 'just dropping by' is one of them.

'It's seriously not,' she says defensively.

'Think of it as fate, you know? You just happen to stop by, and he just happens to be working there today,' says Camila, trying her hardest to persuade me.

'That doesn't make it true! If I genuinely had just casually dropped into Beats Per Minute looking for, of all preposterous things, a record, that would be OK. But I can't start believing my own lie that I'm just at the shop by chance.'

'First, you love music anyway, so why wouldn't you be at a record shop, aside from the fact it ain't the 1970s? Second, if you don't catch him now, who knows when he'll be at work again? Who knows when you'll see him again?' Abi is evidently doing her best to appeal to my sense of drama.

'Or *if* you'll see him again,' says Camila, managing to one-up her.

'Look, if I did do this, what would I even say to him?'

'"Hello", like a normal person. "How are you?", like a normal person. "It was nice to meet you", like a normal person,' Abi says, rolling her eyes like I'm being deliberately slow.

'And then feign surprise that he works there, like a normal person who isn't stalking him,' says Camila.

'So, you *do* think it's stalking! Jesus. You and your terrible advice,' I groan.

'We can't all be blessed with your advice skills, my friend.'

I do want to see Joe. I want to see if he's how I remember him, because I'm scared I've remembered him better than he is. The problem is that I only want to see *him*. I don't want him to see me, and I really don't want to talk to him, because talking to Joe sets a precedent for more talking to Joe, and then it'll have to become a thing I do, when in fact all I want is for him to fall madly in love with me with zero effort on my part. Zero risk equals zero embarrassment. But I know that isn't going to happen. Although it feels easier to not get involved, I'm feeling like a moth to a flame. I know where he is right at this second. The thought of it is making my heart flutter.

A switch flips in my head. 'I'm going to do it.'

'Do you want us to come with you, for backup, like?' asks Abi, always keen to be in the thick of it.

'No – it would be even weirder if I brought bodyguards. And you might say something awkward by accident. The fewer people there, the less chance there is of something awful happening.'

Is this true? I could probably make quite awful things happen all by myself.

'Debatable,' says Camila, grinning. She knows I'm not famed for my smooth moves.

'I need optimism, pep and good vibes for my little definitely-not-stalking trip. Wish me luck, pals.'

I haul myself off the bench and start my purposeful stroll up the hill to the shop. I brush my hair as I walk, even though there's not quite enough time to transform myself into a megababe en route. Don't think about it. Be normal. This is normal. Everything is fine, I tell myself as I breathe in and out, in and out, trying to clear my head of stressful thoughts. I'm sure people do much weirder things than this all the time, but also . . . what would I know?

The bright shopfront looms over me as soon as I turn on to the side street. I'm gobsmacked; it just doesn't fit in, and it's so beautiful. It's painted a strong, beautiful vibrant blue, with BPM barely visible in thin black lettering.

I press my hand against the cool glass pane of the door and push it open without giving myself any time to think. As soon as I breach the threshold, I feel acutely aware of the way my body is moving. Is this a normal way to walk? Is this where you normally have your hands when you're walking? Where do you normally hold your gaze when you're not looking for anything or anyone in particular? It hits me now, I should have made notes. 'How to be normal.'

The tinkling bell above the door heralds my extremely normal arrival, so I have no time to figure out my grand plan, because right there, right behind the counter, mere metres from the door, is Joe, looking up from his book to see who is darkening his doorway.

Just seeing him really would have been enough. If I could have just stared at him through the glass and not gone inside, I would have been happy, although I'm extremely aware that would have made me look even weirder. He's so unbelievably cute; I hadn't remembered him wrong at all.

Is it possible he's got cuter? In fact, yes, it is, because he's wearing his glasses. Jesus.

For a few seconds, I just look around. How have I never been here before? It's amazing. It's absolutely crammed with records and CDs, and there's even a bargain bin full of tapes. I guess I've never been here before because, really, who physically owns music any more? But still, it's kind of an incredible place to have on my doorstep. Its walls are covered with sun-faded posters of Bruce Springsteen, Grace Jones, Neil Young. In the afternoon light, everything seems to be filtered through a fine dust. Even though the shop feels like it's bursting at the seams with stuff, everything is actually meticulously ordered and maintained. I try to take in as much of it as I can, but naturally my attentions are divided. Maybe I'll come back another day when he's not working and have a proper nose around. Maybe I'll become a Real Music person.

I'm prepared for the polite *'Welcome to the shop'* smile to signal he has no idea who I am, but it doesn't come. Instead, my heart leaps: it's a real smile; a warm one. He puts down the book he's reading.

'Oh!' I chirp in faux surprise. Now I know he recognizes me, I don't have to pretend I don't recognize him, which at least saves me from one layer of social fraud.

'Hello . . . Emma? Emily?' he ventures, squinting his left eye and cocking his head.

'Yes, that's me. The Emily one. Not the Emma one,' I garble. Idiot. 'Do you . . . Do you work here?'

'I do indeed. My parents have owned this shop for decades, and now I'm attempting to make an honest living by looking after it on quiet days,' he says.

'Oh, that's cool,' I say. I guess it is, really. You could do worse than working in a music shop.

'Except every day is a quiet day,' he says, lowering his voice.

He's not kidding. Aside from me, there's just a random middle-aged man in an anorak poking through the jazz section, occasionally taking a record out, perusing it and replacing it. I don't know what to say in response, so I just let his words hang in the air.

Which turns into a dreaded awkward silence.

'So . . . how can I help you?' Joe says after what feels like an eternity.

Oh God, I haven't prepared for this moment. How *can* he help me?

'My dad found his old record player in the loft yesterday,' I lie smoothly. Where did that come from? Not too shabby, Emily. 'I wanted to take advantage of this . . . new musical discovery and buy a record.'

'Your first ever record?' His eyes light up.

'Yes! I mean, it's not like I've never listened to music

before. Just . . . not a record,' I garble. God, I hope that didn't sound too defensive.

'OK, so no pressure on this purchase at all,' says Joe, grinning.

It's only as he says this that I fully understand I'm going to actually have to exchange my hard-earned cash for a record to legitimize my visit. I know we do have a record player somewhere, probably in the loft, so maybe it wouldn't be a complete waste of money. Even if it is, it's probably worth it for giving me the excuse to chat to Joe. Do I keep it short and just buy something I already know I like so I can get out of here? Or do I use this as an opportunity to bond with Joe?

Don't be a dickhead, Emily. This is going much better than you thought it would. See it through.

Like a sign from the heavens, the anorak man leaves. I guess this means I'm alone with Joe. And Joe is legitimately engaged in helping me. Oh my actual God, I cannot believe my luck.

'OK, so what sort of thing are you looking for?' he asks, eager as a puppy to help me out.

'I hadn't really thought about it . . .' Well, at least I'm not just wall-to-wall lying. I *hadn't* thought about it, because until about two minutes ago, I hadn't invented the need for him to help me.

'This record is for you, right? Or for someone else? I need to know who I'm advising.'

'Right . . .' I say, gazing into his eyes, focusing on the dark lashes . . . much darker than his sandy hair. 'Oh, sorry! I mean, yes . . . I don't mean . . . Right . . . I mean, yes – it is for me.'

Joe smiles, apparently unfazed by my goofery. 'Good, that makes it easier. What sort of thing do you like then? Apart from Talking Heads, I mean.'

My stomach flips with happiness because he's remembered our conversation – but then I feel a wave of panic rush over me. What sort of thing do I like? My mind has gone blank. I listen to music all the time, so why can't I think of anything right now? The seconds are ticking by, and I'm just standing there, heart palpitating and mouth open like I'm waiting for something to happen.

'Um . . . let me think . . .' I say, forcing an awkward laugh. Music. Bands. Songs. Anything. Just say something . . .

When I've stared blankly at him for slightly too long, inspiration finally strikes.

'I like Robyn. And the Knife,' I say, as I remember the last things I listened to on my headphones.

'OK, good,' he says, nodding and smiling encouragement.

I'm blushing furiously now. It could have been worse – I could have said two random bands I don't like at all . . .

or some atrocious novelty record from the 1970s. Small mercies, tiny victories.

I follow him as he shuffles up and down the aisles; he's clearly looking for something. The shop is so small, I keep brushing against things with my objectively huge bum. But the aisles are also so narrow, I can stand right up close to Joe without it being weird. I breathe in his powdery smell, but quietly, so I don't get accused of being a heavy-breathing creep.

'This is what I was looking for,' he says, easing a record out of the tightly packed shelf in the section marked 'L'.

He holds out a record in a white sleeve with three asymmetric pastel-coloured triangles overlapping each other like a mountain range. I don't recognize the artwork. I don't have a chance to take anything else in because he's doing his best attentive salesman impression.

'You don't already have it, do you?' he asks.

Would it be cool if I did? Should I say I do?

'I thought this one kind of made sense because Robyn and the Knife are both Swedish and, uh, so is this guy . . .' He trails off. 'That sounds like really weak reasoning now I say it out loud, but . . . it also kind of makes sense. Or I hope it does. When you listen to it . . . which I hope you do.'

Geography-based music recommendations. It doesn't seem the soundest basis on which to categorize artists, but I'm not about to tell Joe that.

'Yeah, that makes sense,' I lie. I look down at the sleeve. There's no name and no title. 'Uh, what is it though?' I feel stupid for asking, but I feel like I would look stupider if I just took his word for it.

'Yes, I see now that the minimalist cover design doesn't include a name . . . it's called *Oh You're So Silent Jens* by Jens Lekman. I really rate it,' he says, pushing his glasses up his nose then running his fingers through his hair nonchalantly.

I turn it over, as if expecting to learn something from the back. I don't learn anything. If I agree to buy this, will he think it's strange? Like I just took the first thing he suggested? I decide I don't care. I'm too intrigued by what he thinks I'll like to care about whether or not I'll actually like it. I just want to know what goes on in his head – and if he 'rates' this album, maybe I can learn something about him too. Plus the Swedish thing reminds me of Camila, and I'm doing all I can to feel close to her at the moment.

'I'll take it.'

'Well, that was easy,' he says cheerily, as he rounds the counter to ring up my purchase.

'I guess so. Thanks for your help.' I try to sound as Super Chilled Out as possible. I notice that the book lying face down on the counter is *The Brooklyn Follies* by Paul Auster. I make a mental note of it. 'You're clearly a skilled salesman.'

'Thanks, but I don't think so . . .' He gestures around

the shop. 'This isn't really my natural habitat, but I didn't know what else to do with my time, so I'm just going to hang out here with my chair and my book until I can figure out what I'm actually planning on doing.'

I'm learning things about Joe! I'm talking to Joe! In real life! What a thrill!

'Yeah, it seems like a pretty sweet deal. Except, you know, all that having to deal with the general public . . .' I say.

'You're not so bad mostly,' he murmurs with a wry smile as he transfers my record into a plastic carrier.

Now the record is in my grubby paws, I have no excuse to be here any longer. Time to make a run for it.

'Well, it was a pleasure doing business with you, Joe,' I say. I don't want to leave. I want to stay near him. I want an excuse to just stay here forever. Or at least until the shop closes. But it doesn't come. He doesn't offer it.

'Yes, I hope you enjoy it. Let me know what you think,' he says.

How? How am I supposed to tell him if I love it – or that I hate it so much, I'm using it as a dinnerplate? Again, he doesn't offer a suggestion.

'I will do. Bye, then . . .' I say as I back out of the shop.

Instantly I feel dejected. So I saw Joe. I talked to Joe. So what? What do I have to show for it? A record I didn't even want? A record I possibly can't even play because who even

75

knows where the record player is. All I want is to see him again, but I only just saw him. Surely I can't keep contriving reasons to go in there. It feels like I wasted an opportunity somehow, but what did I think was going to happen? He was going to declare his undying love for me over the Punk A–F section? Nope.

As I walk to the bus stop, it occurs to me that I don't even know his last name. At least there's something I can do about that – some light internet research, if you will. It's not that weird. All I have to do is search for 'Beats Per Minute Croydon owners', then I can find out his parents' names, which means I can find out his last name. I pull out my phone.

A hop, skip and a jump on the old internet later, I discover that the object of my affection is called Joe Marshall. Wow, what a rare and beautiful name. Even I can't pretend it's exciting, and it's going to make my next task all the more difficult. I open Facebook and type in J-O-E M-A-R-S-H-A-L-L. Against all odds, he appears first. A couple of the guys from Alexander Hall are mutual friends, bless them. I scroll up and down the page, looking for . . . well, I don't know what exactly. But his page is pretty private. His profile photo is cute though. Of course it is; it's a photo of him. Cute Joe looking cute playing a guitar. I'm about to enlarge it when—

'Oi, look where you're going!' splutters some obnoxious middle-aged man in a suit who had the gall to bump into me, a person who he could surely see was not looking where they were going, and is now harassing me about it.

'Oh my GOD, chill out?' I shout back.

'Fat bitch,' he spits.

Of course he does. It's the default insult. The insult to rule all insults. I can't argue back, because it's true – I am fat. Suit loser wins this round. Way to harsh my buzz, suit loser. Even though the insult doesn't come as a surprise, it still hurts. It still makes people stare at me, pity me, internally agree with him, decide yes, I must have done something wrong, even if that something is just the crime of being fat.

I stomp the rest of the way to the bus stop, humiliated.

Safely installed on the bus, I put my earphones in and decide to do something good for myself. I begin to read one of my books for my English class, even though I really, really cannot be bothered with *Tess of the d'Urbervilles* right now (or ever). Not least because it reminds me of the fact that I need to start thinking about what I'm going to do next year, which universities I'm going to apply for, if I'm going to study English or not. I try to focus – I can think about all that another time. But try as I might, I still have to read the first page three times – all I can think about is Joe. His soft-looking, brown-sugar hair. His tortoiseshell glasses. His mild voice . . .

As I'm nearing my stop, I check Facebook again. A notification pops up. 'You and Joe Marshall are now friends.' At first, my heart leaps just seeing his name . . . but . . . how have we become Facebook friends? A wave of horror freezes me in my place. Oh no. Oh no, oh no. In my surprise at being shouted at by the man on the street, I must have . . . Oh God – I must have accidentally clicked 'Add Friend' on Joe's profile. I want the bus seat to swallow me up. I must have added him literally minutes after I left the shop! How keen can a person look? Somehow this feels more humiliating than getting called a fat bitch by a stranger on the street. All I can do is take this as a lesson from the cosmos: Do. Not. Internet. Stalk.

# CHAPTER SEVEN

'Weekend in the Dust' –
David Byrne and St. Vincent

More than two weeks have gone by since I went to Beats Per Minute, and I haven't seen or spoken to Joe once. I can't help wondering if my technological mishap has contributed to this. Any hope I had of the accidental Facebook add sparking some kind of communication from him was in vain: radio silence. It's agony. Absence is making my heart grow extremely fond. I know I said no internet stalking, but it would be a big fat lie if I said I didn't check his Facebook every day. For what? For clues of course. That's all you're ever looking for when you go a-creeping on someone's page. Clues about what they're doing and, more importantly, who they're doing it with. Just hints, you know. Evidence about his life, his world. I want to know all about him. I want to know what kind of person he is . . .

I discover he's mostly been at work. His sister (at least, I assume it's his sister – it would be too weird if his girlfriend had the same last name as him, right?) tagged him in a status at the cinema on 20 September. He posted a link to a Robert

Palmer video on 26 September, saying that he died on this day some years ago and that he was 'underrated'. Note to self: get extremely into Robert Palmer.

Against this backdrop of zero communication, I've at least had the record. I made my dad go up into the loft and dig out the record player I correctly suspected was lurking up there. I listen to the record again and again, fuelling my crush. I lie on my bed, listening, listening, listening. This record has filled the gap, letting me follow Joe in my imagination. My favourite song on the album, 'Maple Leaves', starts, and I can see his face. I can smell his warm, soft scent from the record shop. I wonder how he feels when he hears it. It's big and beautiful and expansive and sounds old and new at the same time. It sounds like autumn. It sounds like nostalgia and possibilities and looking back and looking forward and not knowing what you're doing. I lose myself in the song. Track two of the only record I own: Joe Marshall-approved *Oh You're So Silent Jens*. Two weeks is a long time when all you have is one record and the odd status update to nourish your crush. I gnaw the icing off the sides of a pink fondant fancy and think about my next move.

It's Saturday morning, and I'm meeting Camila at the cinema to see some romcom around lunchtime . . . Maybe . . . just maybe . . . No, kill that thought. But . . . I could . . . I could pop into the shop . . . just to see if he was around. It wouldn't be far out of my way. It wouldn't be the weirdest place for me to turn up . . . I shouldn't. But I could. Now the idea has occurred to me, I can't make it un-occur. Oh, Emily. You big weirdo.

I dress carefully, settling on a denim pinafore dress over a chunky navy sweater with tights and flat cherry-red Dr Martens shoes. As I deliberate over black or brown eyeliner, I catch my reflection in the mirror. I set both the eyeliner pencils down. Who are you kidding? As if this guy – this cute, interesting, intelligent guy – is going to notice whether you're wearing black or brown eyeliner. Nope! These kinds of thoughts will not do. This is not what I need right now. I need verve and pep and positive mental attitude, not to behave like a whiny baby because Ryan bruised my ego.

I choose black.

An hour later, I'm pushing open the door to Beats Per Minute. No going back now. As soon as the door swings open and the bell chimes, I see not Joe, but a middle-aged man behind the counter. Of course Joe isn't here. The man smiles at me, but it still feels like my heart has dropped out of my chest. I hadn't actually thought through as far as the possibility of Joe simply not being here. He does do other stuff, you know, Emily. He does have a life. He does have other places to be. I just hadn't thought about it.

I feign interest in the new-arrivals section for precisely thirty seconds (I count them, deciding that would pass a reasonable amount of time in the shop) before turning on my heel and heading for the door.

'Emily?'

I spin round, my heart immediately filling up with excitement.

'Oh, hi!' I say. Unlike last time, I'm genuinely surprised to see him. No time to overthink my tone of voice or my body language.

'What brings you here this fine Saturday?' Joe says, wiping his dusty hands down his black jeans. His hands look soft. Clean nails.

I decide honesty is the best policy. Not least because I've been caught off-guard and don't have time to think of a lie. 'I was actually looking for you,' I say, as casually as you can say something like that.

'Oh really?' He furrows his brow. His expression is unreadable.

'Yeah, it's nothing much – I just wanted to say I really love the Jens Lekman record. I've been listening to it a lot.'

'You liked it, huh?' he says, grinning. He looks genuinely happy, like he knows he's done a good job.

'Yeah, I really, really did,' I reply, trying not to faint at the sheer perfection of his smile. 'It's kind of like Arthur Russell but more like . . . straight-up pop, right? Like all the sixties girl-group stuff . . .'

'Uh, yeah, I guess you're right,' he says, as if he's never thought about it before.

There's a pause I don't know how to fill.

'So . . . you just came here to tell me that?' he asks matter-of-factly.

As we stand there in the aisle by the doorway, it's one of those moments where I'm acutely aware of how much space I'm taking up. I shift on the spot, trying to find a position where I look smaller somehow. More petite, more ladylike. There isn't one.

'Yeah. I did,' I say defiantly. Just because it is a weird thing to do, doesn't mean I'm going to let him know I think it's weird too.

'Well, if you—' he begins to say, but he's cut off.

'Joseph! Enough chatting – you've got work to do, haven't you?' calls the man behind the counter, sounding good-natured but firm.

Joe blushes. 'Yes, Dad. I've got work to do,' he says with a huff. Turns out even seriously cute guys get told what to do by their parents sometimes. He turns back to me. 'I guess I should get back on it . . .' he says, looking around as if to offer an explanation.

'Course. I was on my way to meet my friend anyway,' I say.

I want to tell him about 'Maple Leaves'. I want to know if my favourite is his favourite too, or if I'll have to wrap myself up in another song altogether. But we don't have time for an in-depth chat right now.

'Wait. Before you go – I know you added me on Facebook, but I don't use it much,' he says, as he fishes in his jeans pocket and pulls out his phone.

I just stand there as he types something into it, which seems kind of rude as we were in the middle of a conversation.

'There,' he says. 'I've messaged you my number.'

His number. Wow. I have his number. My crush's actual telephone number.

He laughs warmly. 'You can never have too many friends who love music, I guess!'

'Great!' I smile stiffly, turn around and head out of the door. Ugh. It feels like he's twisting a knife in my chest. *Friends*. Of course. Why does that word, which means something so amazing and positive and life-affirming, feel so weak and hollow when it comes from someone you're attracted to? It's funny how much of a difference that word makes. It's not like I *don't* want someone to talk about music with. I just don't want it to be Joe.

Suddenly noticing the time, I dash to the cinema so I'm not late for the film.

The 'new and improved' Camila is waiting for me, cinema tickets in hand. She's wearing a cute sweater and a little denim mini skirt that I've never seen her wear before.

'OK, something just happened, and I need to tell you about it,' I say, slowly. I wish I could just relax into this crush on Joe, accept it for what it is, but I can't.

'Go on.'

'I just went to creep on Joe again—'

'Oh, so this is becoming a regular thing now? After you protested against it so much the first time!'

'No. That's the thing. I don't need to stalk him in person any more because he gave me his number.'

'This is good. This is very good,' Camila says, her eyes lighting up.

'No, it's not like that. It doesn't really mean anything, right?'

'If you say so,' she says.

It's only then I notice she's been messaging pretty much non-stop during our conversation.

'Who are you messaging?' I ask suspiciously.

'Oh, no one,' she says, but she's still typing while looking at me, her thumbs skittering over the keyboard like she can't tear herself away even for a moment.

Red flag. This definitely means 'boy'.

'Come on! I've given you some solid, tangible gossip today: I got a boy's whole phone number. At least have the good manners to tell me who's making you smile,' I say, trying to sound chilled but really freaking out inside. Camila's never had a boy to message before. Something's changed.

She opens her mouth to speak, then closes it instantly, breathes in deeply, and holds her breath for a few seconds. 'Ryan. It's Ryan. You know him?' she says, finally, smiling coyly and sighing like a lovesick cliché.

I can feel the colour drain from my face like in a cartoon.

'Ryan Russell?' I ask. There is no other Ryan. I feel sick. I was too fat for him, but newly transformed Camila's just right.

'Yes! Isn't he great,' she says, but she doesn't wait for me to confirm or deny either way. She just smiles at me with that earnest, sincere smile of hers. 'I just don't want to jinx it, you know? I like him a lot! We met at reading group, and we've been messaging.'

Yes, I can see you've been messaging, I think to myself. Right in front of me.

'I know it's early days and all that. Please don't tell anyone yet.'

'Um, sure – I won't tell.' Spreading the fact that I'm now the very last remaining girl in the world with no boyfriend and no one interested in me? No thanks. 'He seems really nice. Good for you.'

'Thank you,' she says and squeezes my arm. 'I just feel so much better these days. Like I'm ready to date, you know?'

Inside the auditorium, we settle into our seats, and I watch as Camila messages throughout the adverts, intermittently giggling and making a half-arsed attempt to engage me in conversation so she doesn't seem rude. I've zoned out of the cinema and zoned into feeling rubbish. Obviously this isn't all bad: I should be happy for her. But *I feel so much better these days* is barely coded *I feel so much thinner these days.* No wonder she's ready to date: she finally has a body that makes her the kind of girl guys want on their arm. And not just any guy! Specifically a guy that literally one hundred per cent rejected me because my fat body was repulsive to him. Thank God she doesn't know that. He had better not tell her. I'll kick him in the balls if he does. Camila has every right to be happy. She does. I just wish that her version of happy didn't feel so bad to me.

When the film finishes, I'm about to suggest we go for ice cream, but turns out Camila's got places to be.

'I'm . . . well . . . I'm going to Ryan's,' she says.

She looks overjoyed, and I hate myself for having any pangs of jealousy at all.

'Oh. So, are you two, like, a proper thing then?' I ask.

'I hope so,' she says, nibbling the skin on her lip. 'I mean, you never can really tell where you're at with guys, but we've been making out a lot . . . I would definitely, you know . . . if he wanted to.'

'Oh. Well, I guess just make sure you're ready. It seems pretty quick.' Who am I to be giving sex advice? I guess it's not so much advice as a self-preserving delay tactic. I feel guilty knowing this is my angle on the whole situation, but honestly, I can't be the last virgin standing.

'I guess . . . but when you know, you know,' she says decisively.

I say goodbye to Camila outside the cinema, where she stays to wait for Ryan. I desperately do not want to cross paths with him, especially not with Camila in her new loved-up state. I wonder if I'll ever really know what that feels like.

# CHAPTER EIGHT

'We Share Our Mothers' Health' – The Knife

Ryan and Camila have lasted three weeks so far. And to be honest, they do make a pretty nice couple. I have to admit, they make more sense together than me and Ryan would. Camila is happy, and I'm feeling less embarrassed about being brutally rejected by her now boyfriend. September has bled into October, and he still hangs about outside the school gates at the end of most days, waiting all excited for her to run into his arms.

Me? Less film-script romance, more the romantic wasteland of a maudlin indie song. And I'm finding myself thinking about my body more. Worrying about it more, I guess. Not because I care, really, but because I worry about how it's judged by people around me. Because that's something I can't change.

As I walk home from school, I think about how Ryan's rejection has kind of burrowed into my brain. And not seeing Joe for the past two weeks isn't helping. I think about him, and I really want to see him – but then I decide I don't want to see him, because although he'd probably want to hang out with me, he'd *also* be totally disgusted by the idea of me fancying him for exactly the same reason Ryan was. Ugh. Boys.

My key is barely in the lock when my mum pounces on me.

'Emily! You're home!'

What's all this about, eh? Something's amiss.

'I am indeed. Why are you waiting for me on the doormat?'

'I'm just happy to see you, that's all.'

'Really?'

'Really! How was school?'

I open my mouth to reply, but she's already straight in.

'Oh, and I was hoping you would do something with me tonight . . .' She trails off, looking unsure.

I can already tell it's not going to be a trip to the cinema or a cheeky Nando's. 'Try me,' I say.

'Well, I was thinking of trying . . . um . . . a new weight-loss group,' she says quite matter-of-factly.

It's so obvious she's trying to make herself sound eminently reasonable.

'And what does that have to do with me?' I very much do not want to get involved with this.

'I was hoping I could count on you for a bit of moral support, but if you've got too much going on, that's fine,' she says.

I'm much too easy to guilt trip, and she knows it.

'No, go on.'

'Well, it's only at the church hall around the corner, and I was wondering if you would come with me,' she says.

'Why?'

'Like I said – for moral support.'

'Why me?'

'Because Dad's in town having dinner with his writing-group friends tonight, and I don't know who else to ask.'

'Why can't you go on your own?'

'Because I'm nervous and want someone there to distract me.'

She looks genuinely anxious. Maybe this isn't about me for once.

Mum bites her lip and swallows. 'And because I'm scared about facing the reality of how much weight I've put on,' she adds.

My heart drops, and I can feel the blood rush to my cheeks. The hot feeling of shame as my mum's shame is reflected back at me.

'Ugh, I really do not want to do this,' I say, shaking my head.

'Do it for me,' she whines, bobbing up and down with nervous energy. 'Do it as a favour for your old mum.'

I close my eyes, hoping that when I open them, she'll announce she was only joking. She's not really going to try another destructive, madcap diet; she's not going to plough all her hopes and dreams into what amounts to yet another scam; and she's definitely not going to look to me for approval.

I open them. She's still looking at me expectantly.

'I just don't understand why you have to drag me into it.' I sigh. 'What exactly is it, anyway?'

'It's called the Wellness System,' she says.

Oh, cool. Seems legit – only the worst name you could think of. At least I was right in my suspicions of Mum hiding something weird on the computer.

'It's not like a normal slimming club; it focuses on, well, wellness and health and well-being.'

Oh, I'm sure it's not like a normal slimming club. That's what they all say. 'But the point is you lose weight, right?'

'Yes, I suppose so.'

'Why do you think this time will be different?' I ask.

'Different to what?' She looks confused.

'Different to all the other times you've tried to lose weight.'

'I'm really ready to try this time,' she says with a quiver in her voice.

'So, what? All the other times, you were just messing about?'

Mum shrugs. 'My heart wasn't really in it then. But this time, it's different.'

I sigh. I can't help it. This time will *not* be different. It's just the latest rung in the ever-descending ladder into madness and misery. This is a bad idea, I just know it. But it's my mum's idea. What am I meant to do?

'Please – I really don't want to go to this thing,' I say. This is my last refusal.

Mum looks down at her feet, tracing a pattern on the carpet with the toe of her trainer. 'It's really important to me. I would really appreciate it. You don't know how hard it is for me to do things like this. I'm not confident like you. I wish I was. I wish it was easy for me to bluster into new places and feel on top of things, but it isn't. I need your help, Emily. Please, just come to one meeting with me so I can get myself started.'

I hate myself already because I know I'm about to say yes. I can't stop myself. Even though I don't agree with her, at least now I understand where she's coming from, why she feels this way about her body. Women's bodies are always pored over and scrutinized, but it feels like there's nowhere to hide when you're fat. I suppose it wouldn't kill me to go along with her, just this once. The Wellness System. I hate it already.

'Oh, all right,' I say. *Mistake, mistake, mistake* flashes in my head like a big neon sign.

'Emily, you're such a good girl! Thank you!' she says,

93

hugging me. 'The meeting starts in half an hour. Let me just get my things together and make sure I've got cash . . .'

A split second later, she's off rummaging around in the living room. As I watch, I wonder how much money she's put into all these fad diets over the years. Frittering away my inheritance on juice cleanses and colonic irrigations. I don't want to know the answer. Think how many lipsticks or dresses or gig tickets that would buy. It's painful.

When we arrive, the church hall smells like . . . a church hall. Orange squash, biscuits, dust – the usual. It's a wild hive of activity, split up into three main areas: the first, several lines of chairs facing no one in particular (at the moment); the second, a long trestle table covered in brightly wrapped packaged food; and the third, lines of people queuing to be weighed at a couple of sets of scales. Tonight's the night for the Wellness System.

I shuffle in with my mum, burning with profound embarrassment. It's not that I think it's embarrassing to go to the Wellness System; it's more that I'm ashamed that people here will be looking at me and seeing another unhappy fat person. I hate that I'm adding to the numbers here, hate that I'm encouraging people to feel like this about themselves. I feel like even by turning up, I'm saying, 'Yes, you're right. I should change. You should change.' Is that what I'm saying? Is now the time for me? I never wanted this before, but now . . . I don't know. I hate that in a moment of weakness, I caved, and now I'm here and thinking these thoughts.

'Are you feeling all right? You look a bit peaky.' Mum presses a hand against my forehead to, I suppose, feign checking for a temperature. I wonder if she's already looking for an excuse to leave.

'I'm fine – loving life.' I sigh. I'm the picture of a sulking teenager.

We're standing around – looking conspicuously new, lost and uncomfortable – when a pretty, petite blonde woman swoops on us.

'Hi! I'm Sharon, and I'm the area leader for the Wellness System,' she says with a massive fixed smile that comes across more like a grimace. 'Congratulations on taking control of your destiny. You're new, aren't you?' She's clearly delighted at the presence of fresh, fatty meat. Gammon. Or pork belly.

I let Mum do the talking. I don't want this woman to think I'm in any way actively participating in her shenanigans.

'Yes, we are new here. I'm Helen, and this is my lovely daughter Emily, and we would like to join today,' Mum says very quickly, twisting her bracelets and not looking at me once. The snake! Does she really think I'm going to fall for this? Does she see it as some kind of intervention?

'Well, that's just wonderful,' simpers the boss lady. 'This is the first day of the rest of your life.'

'No, no, no.' I shake my head and smile. 'In fact, as my mum well knows, I'm just here for moral support.'

'Are you sure? It doesn't look like it would do you any harm . . .' Sharon says brightly, fixed smile still frozen on her thin face.

Screw you, Sharon.

'I'm really fine just the way I am,' I say defiantly. Awkwardly, but defiantly.

'Come on, Emily,' implores my mum. 'It would be for your own good. I'm only encouraging you because I care about you.'

'No way. I'm sorry.' I'm not sorry at all.

'But we're already here, you might as well,' she tries again.

Like I'll fall for that. 'I'm only here because you dragged me here! This isn't about me.'

'Em. Can I call you Em?' Sharon ventures.

My face should tell her she most certainly cannot, but still she continues.

'Look, Em. This could be a wonderful opportunity to transform you into the young woman you were always meant to be. This is a really significant step, you coming here tonight. I know you're scared, but take my hand, and we can begin this journey together.' She holds out her hand.

I slowly look down at it and then back up at her eyes in sheer disbelief. She quickly withdraws it. God loves a trier, and Sharon is trying hard. It's so absurd that even in my extreme rage, I can't help but laugh. I only half manage to suppress it, and it comes out as a choked cough. Sharon looks at me as if I'm contagious. Mum just glares at me, but I'm not in the mood to be polite.

'Well, I can see I'm not going to get anywhere with Em . . . but, Helen, it's just wonderful to have you here tonight. Now let's get you registered so we can do your first weigh-in!' Sharon is galvanized, in her element, ready to go. My rejection clearly didn't sting too badly.

Sharon leads my mum over to the trestle table covered in food, where there's another woman guarding a box of record cards like it's some kind of treasure chest.

'A new member, Sally!' says Sharon, doing jazz hands as she approaches the table.

Sally brandishes a clean record card for my mum to fill out. My mum's brow is furrowed, deep in concentration, properly in the zone. Then it's her big moment. She's led to a weighing station, where the queue has died down as everyone has migrated to the rows of chairs. Despite my annoyance, I try to give my mum an encouraging smile, but she doesn't see me. This clearly means a lot to her, even if I think it's totally bogus.

While Mum's facing her Moment of Truth, I peruse the table displaying the Wellness System-branded food for sale. I instantly understand that despite all its crowing about 'health' and 'wellness', this is a pure money-making weight-loss thing. All the food is un-delicious replacements for delicious things. You can still eat cookies and cakes and spaghetti carbonara! Just . . . an anaemic version. Everything good and fun and tasty in any given food is replaced with artificial colours and sweeteners and additives, which I guess is fine in itself, but . . . why all the *wellness* chat? Why can't they be upfront about what they're doing? Why do they have to couch it in such slippery terms that aren't even true?

My musings are interrupted by the reappearance of my mum, who looks a lot like someone has died.

'God, I've really let myself go,' she says, nibbling her lip.

I knew this was a bad idea.

'No, you haven't.' I sigh. 'You look great.' I want to soothe her, but I know it's pointless.

'I don't – I look awful. I feel awful. I hate it. At least I'm doing something about it though. Come on – the meeting's about to start.'

And with that, my mum frogmarches me across the hall to the rows of folding chairs where everyone has congregated. Meeting? I thought we had done the meeting. I thought *this* was the meeting. What horrors lie in store for us now?

We take our seats somewhere in the middle near the front, as my mum doesn't want to miss a single word. I look around at the other attendees. They're a mixed bunch: a few men, but mostly women; some young people, but mostly older. I am the youngest person here by a long way.

Sharon takes the stage. It feels appropriate that we're in a church hall because she's adopted the air of a benevolent vicar.

'Good evening, everyone, and a very warm welcome to you. I hope you've had a very successful week and you've seen some big losses on the scales tonight!' she simpers. She sounds like a children's TV presenter. 'Although, I know some of you haven't been so good . . . I'm looking at you, Orla!' She nods her head and pouts at a woman who looks like she's usually pale but is now beet red, her mouth an open 'O' of consternation. Poor Orla. Naughty Orla – letting herself live. 'But don't be discouraged! Tomorrow is a brand-new day! Take my advice and drink a glass of water before every meal! In fact, drink a glass of water whenever you're hungry!'

'What, so you can faint and piss yourself at the same time?' I mutter under my breath.

'Shh!' Mum hisses, elbowing me in the ribs.

Enough is enough. 'Mum, I love you, but I'm outta here.' And with that, I quietly slip out of the hall to go and wait for her on a bench outside.

That kind of talk is completely poisonous. I'm not going back in there. How could Mum think she could trick me into buying into this? Why does she want this for me so badly? Is it only because she wants it for herself? I sit on the bench until people start filing out, all looking a bit despondent. When my mum appears, she's not so much morose as furious.

'Emily Daly, I did not raise you to be a rude little monster,' she says, clearly fuming.

'You can talk! You lured me here against my will, under false pretences, with a sob story that I believed because I'm an idiot, but now *I'm* the monster!' She is truly outrageous. It's as if she's created her own reality. I bet in her mind, I'm completely desperate to lose weight, and I begged her to bring me.

She gasps. 'A sob story?! You're unbelievable! I was doing this for your own good.'

'So I keep hearing.'

'I just thought that what with Camila looking so nice these days, you might want to do the same.'

Her words linger in the air. A lump forms in my throat.

I've been ambushed, and it's 'for my own good'. I'm meant to be *grateful*?

We stalk home in silence. There will be no films and fondant fancies tonight.

As soon as we arrive home, Mum springs into action, riffling through the kitchen cupboards, pulling things out and putting them on the worktop. I decide it's easier to just let her go for it, and I entertain myself by perusing the Wellness System's reading material. The basic vibe is . . . well, reading the handbook, I'm struggling to figure out what the logic is at all. Except that anything delicious is banned, I guess? There are glowing testimonials by lots of thin white women about they have *'much more energy!'* since starting 'the System', how their *'skin looks so much clearer!'* and how they're *'sleeping so much better!'* But every single testimonial also contains a little star with a number in the middle to show how much weight each quoted woman has lost. The numbers are wild, exaggerated, obscene. They make no sense.

I'm beginning to see how Mum could have been drawn in by all this. I see why, right now, she's going through boxes of cereal and sorting them into 'acceptable' and 'unacceptable' piles. This bad dieting energy has been let into our house, and I know I won't be safe from it. I know it's going to pollute my home just at the time when I'm feeling weird and wobbly (metaphorically) and vulnerable after getting knocked back the one and only time I tried it on with a guy.

I wait until she's finished her sweep of the kitchen, go in to make myself an omelette, take it upstairs, and hole myself up in my room for the evening. I plough through my food while checking my phone. Within seconds, I discover that the group chat has been aflame tonight – clearly something's been going on. I scroll back up to the origin of the excitement . . .

Ella

**E** LADS LADS LADS –
you'll never guess what!

Sophia

**S** What, babe?

Camila

**C** What?

Abi

**A** Today is Nigerian Independence Day,
I already know.

Ella

**E** Guess.

Abi

**A** No.

Camilla

**C** This had better be good.

Abi

**Come on!**

Ella

**Fine. Cheers for ruining my game, but I'll tell you anyway.**

Sophia

**Go go go.**

Ella

**My parents are away this weekend!!!!!!**

Abi

**YAAAAAAAS!**

Camila

**Party time????**

Ella

**Party time!**

Abi

**Gonna message Oliver right now brb #zerochill**

Ella

**Who needs chill when you can have a party!**

Sophia

**I'll get my dad to buy us some booze from the ol' cash and carry.**

Shh no. Don't ask your dad.
Our parents talk to each other! I'm keeping the party on the downlow – your dad will want to know what the booze is for, and then we're screwed. I'll sort it, no worries, babe.

K.

What about bangers?
We need bangers!

We need to end Ryan's run of being default DJ at every party because no one else steps up. Sorry for dunking on your bf, Camila.

No, it's fine. I actually think you're right.
PLUS! I know someone.

Who?

Yeah what the hell cool DJ do you know, Fosh?

Camila

**C** She's 5 ft 10, light brown hair, ass of an angel.

Ella

**E** OMG, YES – girls to the front.

Abi

**A** Speaking of which, where is she?

Sophia

**S** Stalking that Joe dude maybe?

Ella

**E** How can she forsake us like this at such an important moment?

It's nice to know I'm missed when I'm not around, I guess. Now's my cue to jump in . . .

**E** Excuse you I was ACTUALLY at a slimming club.

Abi

**A** ????

Ella

**E** Give Emily back her phone whoever this is.

**E** No – it's really me, I swear. I had to go with my mum. She literally tricked me :((((

Bleak. I'm sorry.

Yeah, dark. But how do you feel about your new job?

Yeah are you in or . . .

You want me to have sole control over the music All Night Long, as Lionel Ritchie would say?

Yeah, man.

All right, I can deal with that. No pressure, etc.

No there's quite a lot of pressure.

Don't say that. I'll definitely choke.

You got this.

Glad we've settled this. You gonna invite Joooooooe?

Urrrrgh. Am I? Am I going to invite Joe? Even if we're firmly in the friend zone, it would still be nice to have him there. Maybe if I don't invite him, someone else will. Someone invited him to Ben's, after all. This is a really good excuse to talk to him. But would it be weird if I did it? Would it be decidedly un-chill?

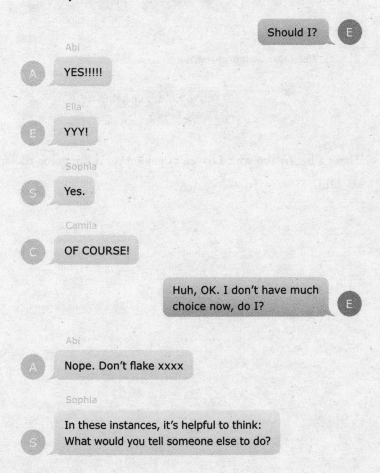

**Should I?** E

Abi
A **YES!!!!!**

Ella
E **YYY!**

Sophia
S **Yes.**

Camila
C **OF COURSE!**

**Huh, OK. I don't have much choice now, do I?** E

Abi
A **Nope. Don't flake xxxx**

Sophia
S **In these instances, it's helpful to think: What would you tell someone else to do?**

You would want you to ask him out if you weren't you.

YEAH! You know it baby!

Asking him to go is one thing. Asking him OUT is another.

Well start with that then!

You're right. I've got to do it. I'll ask him.

That's a lie, by the way. I haven't decided yet if I'm going to ask him.

# CHAPTER NINE

'Fighting Talk' – Everything but the Girl

I finally decide to take the plunge as I'm walking home from the bus stop after school the next day. It's a crisp, clear October afternoon, and I am feeling good about being alive. The first month of my final year of school has passed without catastrophe (tick), it's coat weather (tick), and I'm feeling less completely out of control of my crush on Joe (tick). Accepting he's probably never going to fancy me and keeping my distance has left me feeling calmer. This is the kind of mood you should make decisions in.

I stop for a moment on the corner of my street, close my eyes, and attempt to formulate the perfect message. That's right: it's time for baby's first message to Joe. I've tried to keep my distance from him, play it cool, and not 'just happen' to drop by the shop again. Now I'm going to use the number he gave me instead. Like an adult.

*Hey*, I type. Is 'hey' more casual than 'hi'? Yes, I think it is. OK. *Hey, I was wondering* . . . No, delete that. 'Wondering' is only one step below 'thinking', and we all know it's weird to think about people. My fingers go into rapid-fire mode, typing out a message:

> Hey, Ella's having a party on Saturday. You should come!

I press send before I can think about it.

As I walk through the door, I immediately notice the table is set for five for dinner tonight. I groan, my positive mental attitude of ten minutes ago evaporating as I realize that Auntie Isobel and her boyfriend Weird Dennis are coming over today. Unable to face the sheer horrific enormity of this prospect, I go straight upstairs so I can put Pixies on loud enough that when the doorbell goes, it's not completely implausible that I wouldn't have heard it. Every little helps. The worst part is, Aunt Isobel used to be cool. But her decision to have a relationship with Weird Dennis is completely inexplicable. Tonight, let's play Weird Dennis bingo: if he mentions my weight, the fact he's been to prison (more on that) and my dad's status as chef, cleaner and child-rearer, I will consider it a full house. If he tries to talk to me about Bitcoin, or any kind of 'cryptocurrency' or actually anything that begins with the word 'crypto', then it's bonus points.

So, the prison thing. Dennis likes to tell people he's been to prison. He hasn't. Dennis is the most boring, middle-class white guy on the planet, and he desperately wants to give himself an edge. He sees himself as a freedom fighter, an internet outlaw, a persecuted minority. He calls himself a hacker, but really he just perpetrated a huge data breach in his old job, the police got involved, and he was let off with a caution. He did not go to prison. He thinks he's literally the only person who has ever used the internet, and there's absolutely no way anyone could check up on his story, but obviously I looked up the company he used to work for, found news stories about the 'crime' and – guess what – no prison. Oh, best bit is, Dennis isn't even his real name. He just calls himself that because he's a prickly weirdo about 'security'. Imagine rebranding yourself in adulthood and *choosing* to become a Dennis. Not Antelope or Quark or Velour or Prince. Just Dennis.

My phone vibrates. My heart leaps in my throat. Surely Joe hasn't replied that quickly? But no: it's just my dad texting me from downstairs.

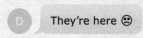

Dad

D   They're here 😟

Make no mistake: the sad face is entirely for Dennis. Grudgingly I drag myself down the stairs and into the living room. Auntie Isobel is wearing a hot-pink satin shirt dress that looks amazing on her tall, curvaceous figure. She beams at me.

'Aaaah, my beautiful niece! I've missed you so much!' she says as she presses me to her chest and strokes my frizzy mane. 'I love your hair this length. You look so lovely.'

She fusses and coos over me until we're rudely interrupted by Weird Dennis himself, returning from the kitchen with a wine glass in each hand.

'Hello, Emily,' he says, awkwardly kissing me on each cheek.

'Hello, Dennis,' I reply, trying to suppress a shudder at coming into physical contact with him.

Dennis is pretty good-looking: imagine an old Hollywood actor transformed into a boring English guy who works in IT. Burt Lancaster by way of Essex. How are men allowed to get away with having mediocre personalities and yet date resplendent, majestic women like my aunt?

We sit around nibbling nuts and chatting (while my mum sips water and looks mournfully at the delicious salty snacks) as my dad puts the finishing touches to dinner. My aunt asks lots of questions about how Katie is getting on in Manchester, if I've thought about what I'm going to do next year, if Mum is up to date with a cop show they both watch. Dennis is getting fidgety, annoyed at the lack of attention.

As soon as we fall silent for a few seconds, the brief interlude is long enough for him to pipe up with his low-quality small talk, and I'm not going to let him get away with it.

'Emily, made up your mind about uni next year?' he says, he clearly hasn't been listening. He tugs the cap off a bottle of beer with his teeth. I suppose he thinks it looks macho rather than idiotic.

'Um, no, not really. I can't make my mind up . . .' But I'm sure I can think of someone who wants to give me a ton of advice about it.

'Well, make sure you get yourself a marketable skill,' he says, nodding sagely. 'There's no point otherwise.'

'I'm thinking I'll probably just stick with English, since that's what I'm good at,' I reply with forced cheeriness. I'm not interested in his career advice.

'Ah, you'll regret that when you're still living at home at the age of thirty!'

I don't reply, forcing an awkward pause, but in mere seconds, he's ready to go again.

'So, Helen, your sister tells me you've started on a new diet? Good for you,' he says.

No, he doesn't so much say as bark. I want to die already. Who asks people stuff like that?

'Yes, it's tough, but it seems to be going well so far,' Mum replies.

You can virtually see her martyrdom forming a halo around her head.

'No chance of getting you on that, eh, Emily?' Dennis winks in a way I assume is meant to be charming and roguish.

'What do you mean?' I'm feigning ignorance. I know it'll wind him up.

'Pardon?' says Dennis.

'I'm asking what you mean by that. What you're . . . trying to say. Because I don't understand.'

'Oh, I'm not trying to say anything,' he splutters, attempting a smile, but the panic in his eyes gives him away.

It's working.

'Well is there a reason you directed your comment at me rather than at anyone else?' I ask brightly.

Yes, I *am* trying to force him to explicitly say, 'You are fat, and that is bad.' Is it petty? Absolutely. But is it any worse than pressuring teenage girls into worrying about their weight because you're annoyed they don't worry about it? Absolutely not.

Mum and Auntie Isobel are shifting in their seats but say nothing: Mum, because she's obviously on Dennis's side; and my aunt, because I think she's enjoying the showdown.

'I . . . I just mean . . . maybe you could stand to lose a bit of weight,' he ventures, deciding to fully commit to his bigotry.

I gasp in mock horror.

'Are you in the habit of bullying teenage girls about their weight? Vulnerable young women under constant pressure from the media and advertising and the fashion industry to conform? You really want to add to that, eh?' I'm enjoying poking him.

Just as he's grasping for a witty riposte, he's saved by the bell, and Dad calls us through for dinner. Dennis basically runs out of the room.

'Never change,' Isobel whispers in my ear as we file into the dining room.

'I don't plan to,' I reply, shaking with fury yet adrenalized from my victory.

We sit down to eat at our wooden dining table, which Mum has decorated with twinkling tea lights. Dad has made smoked mackerel pâté with crusty bread (for everyone except Mum, who has concocted some limp Wellness System-approved salad). I attack the layer of clarified butter on top of the pâté. I'm going to enjoy this. I'm most certainly not going to let Dennis's bullying put me off my food, especially when it's this delicious.

'Doesn't that get you down a bit, Michael?' asks Dennis, nodding his head towards the opposite wall.

'What's that?' asks my dad, looking bemused.

'Seeing that every day – being reminded of your former glory?' Dennis is looking down at his plate as he speaks, determined to be provocative but not actually make eye contact with anyone to face what an idiot he's being.

We all understand now: he's talking about the large framed poster hanging on the wall behind the table. It looks like a vintage circus poster, but it isn't; it was just designed that way. *Bear Trap* it says, above a stylized rendering of a brown bear rearing up on its hind legs. 'By Michael Daly' is printed below in tall letters. Once upon a time, my dad wrote a play about economics and politics and relationships that was very successful and very popular, and for a short time, he was very successful and very popular too. He has spent the past two decades trying to follow it up.

'Actually, I feel like my glory has never really ended. It came as a surprise to me that *Bear Trap* did so well. I suppose I've been dining out on that ever since,' he replies.

Dad is truly blessed with a temperament that resists rising to Dennis's bait.

'Inspiration hasn't struck recently, though?'

My dad sighs and puts his fork down.

'Well, I have a lot of projects that I've started, but nothing has really given me that spark I need to see it through. It's hard to keep up momentum on something you're not really interested in. And it's not like I've been wasting my time since *Bear Trap*.' He smiles at Dennis, perfectly good-natured.

'Quite right! You haven't,' says Auntie Isobel warmly. 'You've learned to cook better than most TV chefs! I remember when you first met Helen, and you could barely boil a carrot. Now look at you.'

But it's no use. She can't reroute the conversation because Dennis isn't done yet.

'You're a braver man than I, Michael,' he says.

Well, obviously that's true, but it's clear this is only another backhanded compliment.

'Oh yes?'

'It takes bravery to let your wife make all the money while you stay at home with the kids. Very . . . modern.' Dennis smiles wolfishly.

I involuntarily throw my head back and emit a guttural groan. I didn't mean to; I just couldn't suppress it. However, as it's unconventional to communicate only in groans, I now have to say something.

'It's not everyone's life mission to prove how aggressively "manly" they are,' I snap. Even if my dad wasn't a proper angel (which he is), I'm still not going to sit here and listen to this gendered nonsense from Mr Toxic Masculinity. 'Some men can figure their lives out for themselves.'

'Know a lot about men, do you?' He chuckles, looking around the room for support.

I've clearly wound Dennis up, and now it's my turn to be on the receiving end.

No, I know absolutely nothing about men, as my complete lack of progress with Joe is proving. Not really planning on opening up to Weird Dennis about that, though. Aunt Isobel sighs loudly and saves me from having to come up with a suitably witty answer.

'Enough, Dennis. Enough,' she says, rolling her eyes.

Her patience with him is wearing so thin, I can almost smell it. I say a little prayer that next time she comes round, she'll have kicked him to the kerb already.

We eat in silence for a moment. Then Dad lays down his fork and sits looking thoughtful for a moment before finally speaking.

'I do have to hand it to you though, Dennis,' he says. 'Only real men go to prison.'

I choke on my bread.

Dad 1: Dennis 0.

After dinner, I volunteer to wash up so I can avoid any further social time with World's Worst Man. And so I can distract myself from the fact my phone hasn't vibrated once all evening. No reply from Joe, no matter how many times I check. I zone out as I let my hands rise and fall in the warm, frothy suds. My moping is interrupted when Auntie Isobel slinks into the kitchen and comes to stand next to me at the sink.

'Come into the garden with me, keep me company while I have a drink. I like being in your garden, even in the dark. As you know, I don't have one, so even the novelty factor is enough for me,' she says, stroking my hair.

I reluctantly agree, if only to keep her happy, and we go and sit outside on the back step in the cool evening air. A question tugs at my insides, and I let it niggle until I can't keep it in any longer.

'Why do you put up with him?' Oh no. Too far, Emily. You can't just ask people why they like dickheads.

But Auntie Isobel just chuckles and looks at me. 'He can be awful sometimes, can't he? It's only when he's around other people. It's like he doesn't know what to say or can't figure out how to give some kind of appropriate response. He's fine when it's just us.'

'I'll take your word for it.'

'Don't worry – I know he's not *The One*. And yes, I still believe in that even at my advanced age.'

'I don't get it, then. What's the point in going out with him?'

'He's fine for right now, and when I start to find him just too much to bear, I'll move on. I know it seems a strange thing for someone to say, but it's different when you're older.'

'Different how?'

'I've found it doesn't take as much out of me to compromise. I can sort of shrug my shoulders and say that I know people I'm dating aren't perfect, but I know who I am, and they sort of . . . don't make that much difference to me. They're just nice to have, not essential. I'm still me. Which isn't an approach I would recommend to you because, although I know you *feel* like a grown-up, emotionally you're like a tiny little newborn baby, and you should be nourished in exactly the ways you need. And besides, you're a sweet, sensitive soul under all that bluster. I've known you since you really were a tiny little newborn baby. I know you – you can't just shrug things off.'

'So, are you trying to tell me, in a roundabout way, that everything does get better?' I ask, trying to sound sufficiently detached that she won't know I'm asking for a reason.

'I don't want to make promises to you that I can't keep, but . . . honestly, yes. Your twenties and thirties are the sweet spot. It's terrible being a teenager, especially if you want to date boys. They're so beholden to what their friends think, so obsessed with trying to impress each other. Everything gets a lot better once everyone's surer of who they are. It does improve. Promise.' She squeezes my knee.

'It had bloody better.'

'Oh no – what's wrong?'

I sigh. 'It's not exactly a catastrophe. I'm just feeling kind of left out. Everyone seems to know what they're doing except me. I'm worried that by the time things do start happening, I'll be, like, *old*, you know? I don't mean actually old—'

'Like me!' she interjects.

'Exactly. No, that's not what I mean at all. I just mean that it'll be weird that I haven't got all this experience that other people have, and it'll be rubbish and embarrassing. That's my current area of anxiety,' I say.

She sips her wine and thinks for a moment. 'I see what you mean. But you will never regret doing stuff in your own time, even if that's slower than everyone else. There's no point rushing this stuff. You'll only end up getting hurt if you try.'

I think I would love the opportunity to get hurt. Better to have loved and lost than never to have loved at all, and all that.

'Emily . . .' she says, gripping my wrist with her free hand as we stand to head back inside.

I look at her, hoping she isn't about to say something extremely serious. 'Yeah?'

'I just wanted to say I'm sorry that he seems to want to wind you up so much. I was thinking earlier that I should tell him off more, but you do seem to be capable of handling yourself,' she says.

'Oh . . . um, that's OK. He's not your child or your pet, I guess,' I reply.

'It feels like he is a bit. To be honest with you, I can't help thinking that being single might be a nice holiday,' she says, with a wistful look in her eye.

An hour later, as we stand waving goodbye to my brilliant aunt and her dreadful boyfriend, I wonder if it's truly that bad to be single. If I really think about it, I would rather literally die a virgin than have to deal with a man like Weird Dennis—

I feel my pocket buzz. I pull my phone out – and my heart leaps.

Joe

 I'll be there.

# CHAPTER TEN

'The Edge of Glory' – Lady Gaga

If I'm going to make the playlist for Ella's party, I'll have to do it right, no messing. It's the morning of the party, and I'm sitting at my laptop with Ted snuffling around my feet, trying to come up with the perfect assortment and sequence of songs to make a seamless start-to-finish . . . experience. Six hours is kind of a long time, it turns out.

Here's my game plan: start off with stuff that was big over the summer, some recent mainstream fun – a little Sia, a little Drake. Then, move things along to some Blondie, Grace Jones, before segueing into some super-happy irony-free tunes to make people want to dance. Maybe Candi Staton followed by 'Groove Is in the Heart'. 'Yes, that's the one,' I whisper aloud as I feverishly drag songs into a playlist.

Once I've used those to establish that it's time to dance, I can break out the girly pop bangers . . . I'm thinking Carly Rae Jepsen, Katy Perry, Little Mix. Let that danceable pop run for a good hour or so, to really keep the mood up, and then cue some Rihanna to transition into 90s hip hop, peaking with 'Hypnotize' by Notorious B.I.G., which I hold dear in my heart as one of my all-time faves.

Then on to the bad-girl bangers – some Kelis, some MIA, some Nicki Minaj – for the all-important phase of the night where everyone's grinding on each other in the dark. I suppose I'm providing a public service: music to make out to. Once everyone's cooled off a bit, we can dial it back down and end the night with some no-nonsense pop tunes like early Madonna. Perfect. A perfectly curated night of music, if I do say so myself.

That was . . . fun. And *kind of* easy. Maybe I should forego university and become a DJ. Note to self: ask the careers advisor at school about this.

I've taken pride in my task for a reason. Now, obviously I would care about making the playlist good anyway (I want Ella's party to be a success! And I'm going, so of course I want it to be fun!). But if I'm honest, I especially, particularly care about making it good because I don't want Joe to think I'm Bad At Music. Joe being at this party gives everything that extra . . . edge, that extra spark, that extra panic. High stakes. Every time I think about seeing him, my heart properly flutters. I thought that was just a made-up thing, like a way of talking about a thought you have about someone, but it turns out it's real. Thinking about Joe produces that physical sparkle in my chest, and I can't keep it away. It's excitement and it's uncertainty all at once. I'm excited for a thing I don't know, that I can't predict. Don't worry: I know that realistically he has probably given no thought to me at all since I last went to Beats Per Minute. He doesn't need to know he's always on my mind—

'Lunchtime!' Dad calls from downstairs, snapping me out of my daydream.

I head downstairs and find that, like a genius, he's made the perfect autumnal lunch of creamy chicken soup with French bread: the ideal calming antidote to my inner butterflies.

'How's your homework going?' he asks. Because what else would I have been doing on my laptop in my room all morning?

'Yeah, good – just been doing some stuff for English,' I mumble into my soup.

'Are you still reading *Tess of the d'Urbervilles*?' Mum says.

My heart drops as I notice she's eating some kind of clear broth. No bread.

'Alas, yes,' I reply.

'It's such a shame that so many books you girls are made to read are about the punishment of women, or keeping women down,' she says. 'I suppose that's the problem with insisting on you reading "classics" at school – they're all morality tales where the moral is that women should stay virtuous. Whatever *that* means.'

'Wow, yes,' I say. 'I completely agree.'

'So do I, Helen. You would think they'd be more committed to teaching texts that rouse the girls a bit more,' Dad says, looking thoughtful.

'Or at the very least were written by women,' Mum adds. 'Even if their so-called moral message left something to be desired.'

I feel warm inside. I know I can be hard on my mum, with all her judgements of my outfits, with all her hare-brained diets and exercise fads. But every so often, I remember why she's great – and she's great because she cares. She thinks; she has a spark; she has something to say. I just wish she didn't get dragged down by all the body anxiety.

'What . . . What would you recommend I read, then?' I ask, seizing an opportunity to bond with her for once.

'Well, for starters, I heard you saying the other day you've never read *The Color Purple*. And I think you'd enjoy *The Handmaid's Tale*,' she says, putting down her spoon and twisting her bracelets, clearly deep in thought. 'I also think Patti Smith's memoir about her life before she was famous is very striking.'

There's more to Mum, it seems, than meets the eye. I guess there's more to all of us.

I thought it was a super-smart decision to take a bath so I'd feel my best for Ella's party, but I ran the bath too hot, and now I look and feel like a boiled lobster. Even though I know I'll cool down eventually, it feels like I'm going to be overheating forever. Sweaty, fat and pink: exactly how I want to turn up to Ella's later. But after a bit of beautifying, it turns out I actually look pretty good, and my black jersey jumpsuit and trainers combo makes me feel sleek. Maybe not such a disaster after all.

A message illuminates my screen. It's Ella telling me to go to hers early so we can hang out. I email her a link to my playlist and head on over.

'Hiya!' Ella's beaming face greets me as she opens her front door. 'Come in!'

'All right, mate,' I say, hugging her. She's so tiny, like a little sparrow, like I could absorb her into my body with a cuddle.

'I think we're pretty much all ready! Sophia! Emily's here!' she calls up the stairs as we head for the living room.

Sophia descends, scrunching her curls to make the most of them, but she already looks perfect. Dressed in a rough approximation of a skinny black suit with trainers, she's the epitome of cool androgyny, Janelle Monaé style. I don't let my size hold me back in terms of what I wear most of the time, but this is one look that I feel kind of cut off from. But hey, I look and, more importantly, *feel* great this evening. Ready to see Joe again.

'You look amazing, Sophia,' I say.

'Doesn't she?!' squeals an excitable Ella as she squeezes her girlfriend from behind.

'Thanks, bud,' Sophia replies, blushing deeply, like she's still getting to grips with her own coolness. 'You're not so bad yourself. I just looked at your music choices for later, and I think you've crushed it.'

Great relief.

'Oh my God, yes! Thank you so much for doing it,' says Ella. 'It means I have one less thing to think about during the party. Plus, takes it out of the boys' hands for once, doesn't it?'

'Speaking of boys, *please* tell me you invited him,' Sophia says with a nudge.

'I did! Don't worry, I didn't chicken out. He said he would come, so . . .'

'Great stuff!' says Ella, pouring us all a cup of cheap white wine. 'Cheers! So, Emily, are you excited about seeing Joe tonight?' She's like a Labrador puppy with her earnest enthusiasm.

'Honestly, I really don't think he's interested, guys . . .' I say, staring into my plastic cup, wishing I could feel as excited as my friends do.

'First, there's no reason why not,' says Sophia. 'You're awesome. Second, it's just FUN that you're into someone.

You need to stop worrying about this so much! It's a fun and nice thing.' She strokes her girlfriend's short, shaggy hair absent-mindedly.

'It's hard, man. It really is. This whole crush thing has freaked me out,' I say, shaking my head.

But then the doorbell rings, and I don't get a chance to say any more. To be honest, I didn't really know what I wanted to say anyway. I guess I want to know why everyone thinks having a crush is so fun, when really it feels so bleak and embarrassing.

'We get it,' says Ella. 'It's hard. It's stressful. But it's a new thing for you, so of course it's weird, and of course it feels difficult.'

Huh – I'm not usually on the receiving end of other people's wisdom. It feels nice. I see why it's a thing people like getting from me.

Ella smiles. 'We want this to work out for you. Like, that is specifically what we want.'

I look up as Camila walks in and hands over a bottle of supermarket own-brand gin to our hostess.

'Hey ladies!' she coos, fluttering her eyelashes.

She looks incredible, wearing a figure-hugging black dress that, yet again, she would never have worn before . . . before.

'Hello, angel,' I say, rising to greet her. She feels sort of stiff as I hug her, and I notice a hint of tension in her smile as I pull away. It runs through me like a shudder. Maybe I imagined it.

We sit around, sipping our bargain-bin alcohol and chatting until the advertised start time of Ella's soiree. People start to trickle in, then loads arrive all at once, including Ryan, but not including Joe. Camila spends the rest of the evening no more than three feet away from Ryan, who has gone out of his way to avoid me, as if I'm going to attempt to kiss him again in the middle of the living room.

I'm glad I've at least made such an excellent playlist for the night because it means more people are dancing than I've ever seen dance at any other house party. And I need a distraction. I need to not keep glancing at the door every time the bell goes or someone knocks. I need to stop looking around the various huddles of people gathered in groups around the house. I need to stop taking trips to the kitchen for more wine, when really I'm just scanning for Joe's face. Just on the wild, improbable off-chance I missed him coming in. How could I have missed him when my eyes have barely left the door? OK, if I can't actually distract myself, I need to at least look like I'm distracted. It's not good for my image to be pining.

'No Joe?' asks Abi, later in the night when we're all gently twisting and swaying to 'Regulate' by Warren G and Nate Dogg.

I wish my friends didn't already know he was meant to be here. I wish I hadn't told them at all. I wonder if the hot humiliation is actually radiating off me, or if it just feels like you can tell I'm deeply embarrassed just by looking at me.

'No, I guess he couldn't make it,' I say, smiling weakly, although my cheeks are burning. I knock back another gulp of wine.

'Aaaah, mate, I'm sorry,' she says, slipping her long, toned arms around me, letting her braids fall over my shoulder like a comforting veil.

'Thanks, pal. Is everything good with you and Oliver?' I ask, keen to change the subject, to brush it off and leave no trace that it meant anything to me at all.

'Uh, yeah, sure – everything's fine. We really like each other,' she says, looking around, apparently distracted.

'Hi, Abi!' an over-sugary voice crows from behind us.

It's Holly, dressed in a black playsuit and heels. I guess Ella couldn't not invite her when she invited basically everyone else in Croydon.

'Oh, and hi, Emily . . .' she says, curling her lip.

'Hi, Holly – how's it going?' Abi says, resigned to the fact she's definitely going to have to talk to her.

'Oh, all right – you know how it is. Always busy keeping my grades up and keeping the netball team in check, and I assume you saw I got the lead in the pre-Christmas play?'

Holly says, with an air of faux-nonchalance so clearly faux that I say a silent prayer that her acting in the play is even slightly better than this.

'I sure did,' says Abi, all too enthusiastically.

'And I got a Saturday job at Rock, that cool new salon,' she says, taking a sip from her cup of rosé.

To anyone else, I would say cool! Live your dream! Increase your earning potential! Tell me about your work goals and aspirations! But with Holly, I just can't muster the enthusiasm.

'That's great,' says Abi, picking up the slack yet again.

'You still babysitting, Emily?' Holly asks.

She wouldn't be Holly if she couldn't only see her own achievements in the context of 'beating' someone else's.

'Yep – they're great kids. Really easy to look after, and the money's fine . . .' I say. Gross – why am I justifying myself to her?

Holly smiles back, wolfish. 'By the way, Emily. I love your jumpsuit,' she says, looking me up and down.

'Um, thanks?' I say, confused at the rare compliment.

'Yeah, it's like a –' she thinks for a moment – '*sensible* version of mine, isn't it?'

I roll my eyes, and she stalks off to the kitchen.

All of a sudden, I hate myself. I hate the music; I hate my clothes; I hate the party. I hate my mistaken belief that it would all add up to something. What if he *was* here?

What if he had come? What difference would it make? I would still be the pathetic fat girl chasing him at work, stalking him online, inviting him to stuff he doesn't want to go to. I can't believe I ever thought this fantasy might play out like it does for the Camilas or the Abis of the world. People who fit in, or make themselves fit in. Maybe I should try to fit in?

And I wish I could tell you that just at that moment, just when I was most desperate for him to turn up, he walked through the door. I wish I could say that I turned around, and he was there. But I can't.

So, I vow to put him out of my mind. I decide another trip to the kitchen for more wine is in order, even though I'm feeling a bit unsteady on my feet. As I attempt to slink across the makeshift dance floor in the centre of the living room, a hand shoots out and grabs my wrist. It's Camila.

'Ryan told me what you did,' she says, emboldened by an evening of drinking.

Whatever this is about, I'm so not up for it right now.

'What? What have I done?' I ask, in no mood to appease. Is this because I knocked him off his 'Party-Music King' throne? Male pride?

'Are you really gonna stand there and pretend you didn't try to kiss him at Ben's party? That you didn't throw yourself at him?' she sneers.

'Well, I didn't. I don't know how he's spun it, but it was kind of mutual, and nothing happened anyway. To be honest, I don't even know why he bothered bringing it up with you,' I say. 'It seems kind of unnecessary.' All this is true, so why does it sound like a lie when I'm saying it to her? The mere fact that I'm having to justify myself makes it sound untrue.

'He says you pretended you were just having a friendly chat, and then you pounced on him,' she says, her eyes flashing.

'Well, that's not true. I don't know what else to tell you,' I say, as calmly as I can. It's hard to make your voice sound chilled when you're literally having to shout because the music is so loud.

'I knew there was a reason you didn't seem happy for me when I told you we were seeing each other,' she says. 'I knew you were jealous of me.'

Jealous! This is too much. But I know if I say anything, I'll cry. What does she want from me? Does she want me to say *You're right — I wasn't happy for you because I'm jealous that you're going out with Ryan?* Or would she rather just hear the truth? *No, I wasn't happy for you because I'm scared you're living proof that I have to lose weight if I want to get a guy. I wasn't happy that a guy who couldn't even bring himself to kiss me once is finding it so easy to have a proper relationship with you. I'm not happy that I'm getting absolutely nowhere with Joe, and it feels like I've been left behind . . .*

I shake my wrist free of her grasp, but am spared having to come up with an answer because Ryan's appeared from the garden, looking stressed and shifty at the sight of us in tense conversation.

'Oh, sorry to interrupt,' he says awkwardly.

'Not at all – I was just going to the kitchen,' I say, not willing to spend another second in their company.

I stumble towards more wine. My head is throbbing, but I don't care. More wine will help. Unfortunately, Ryan catches up with me before I can get there.

'God, was she having a go at you about . . . the thing?' Ryan says, grimacing.

'Yeah. That's what was happening. So, thanks for telling her, I guess.'

'I'm really sorry! I didn't think it was going to be such a big deal to her, which was stupid of me. It just came up—'

'How? How did it come up? Were you having a conversation about humiliating anecdotes?'

'No! Not at all! Jesus, Emily. It's just . . . kind of embarrassing.'

'I know you find me embarrassing – you don't need to rub it in.'

'No, I don't! That's not what I mean. OK, I'm explaining really badly. It's embarrassing to have to retell the conversation. We were talking about people we think

135

are like . . . attractive. Apart from each other. And I said I always thought you were really cute, and how you and I nearly kissed once, but at the last minute I realized it would make things complicated because I knew I really wanted to ask Camila out when she got home from Sweden.'

I stare at him, open-mouthed. My face flushes red. That's . . . not how I thought it happened. At all. 'OK . . . I guess that makes sense,' I say, swallowing hard.

'Yeah, and now she's got a massive bee in her bonnet about it, like you're some major threat to our relationship. I shouldn't have said anything at all. I'm just sorry that I did.'

'It's OK, Ryan. It's OK. Don't worry about it,' I say, feeling my eyes go fuzzy with the alcohol as I lazily clap him on the shoulder and send him on his way, back to Camila.

In the kitchen, under the harsh strip lights, I lean against the counter and wallow in my own confusion. Just because Ryan didn't reject me because I'm fat, does it actually change anything? Does one person thinking I'm cute mean that things are actually going to be any easier with Joe? *Joe.* Where is he, anyway? Maybe I should message him? As I take out my phone, I wonder if I'm about to vomit. Instead of more wine, I do the right thing for once and pour myself a glass of water. I won't message Joe until I've drunk the water. That's a good compromise.

'You all right, Em?' says Oliver, limping in on a crutch,

his ankle bandaged from a rugby injury. He's the only person who gets away with calling me Em. I guess the fact he doesn't speak much means that I let him say what he wants when he does.

'Yeah, sure, I'm fine,' I slur unconvincingly as he rummages around in the fridge for a can.

He looks me over as if to assess whether I'm drunk enough to need caretaking.

I'm not.

'Whatever you do, mate, don't drink and dial,' he says, nodding at my phone in my hand. He cracks a broad, white smile and hops off, the can tucked safely under his arm.

He's right. That's some damn good advice.

It's Sunday morning, and I'm squinting up at my phone, trying not to drop it on my face. I'm tucked up in my bed, and I'm relieved to report I only have a slight headache. I type a message out to Abi.

> Your bf totally saved me from embarrassing myself last night. Tell him he's an angel.

I hit send and let sleep take me over again.

I wake up what feels like minutes later, roused by the

insistent buzz of my phone receiving a message. Most unlike Abi to be awake at this time on a Sunday. But it's not from Abi.

Joe

> Emily, I'm so sorry I didn't come last night. I feel awful (physically/morally) – I have flu, and I kidded myself it was just a cold, but I've basically been asleep for twelve hours straight. It would be cool to hang out with you sometime, though.

My heart feels like it's going to jump out of my chest. Any message from Joe would make me feel like that, let alone one where he says it would be 'cool to hang out'. I'm snoozing no longer. I am officially wide awake. I regret opening the message so quickly because now he'll see that I've read it. Damn. No chance to play it cool. He's online, so I can't mark it unread. If I leave it ages to reply, he'll know I'm attempting to play it cool, which is the least cool thing of all. What do I want to say, though? He didn't actually suggest when to hang out, or what 'hang out' means, or why he thinks it would be 'cool'. I'm overthinking it. It clearly wasn't the worst message to receive.

My message to Abi feels one hundred per cent truer now – would I have received this kind of reply from Joe if

I'd drunkenly demanded to know where he was and why he hadn't shown up? Nope. I cringe just thinking about it, and I didn't even do it.

Thank God for Oliver.

# CHAPTER ELEVEN

'Are "Friends" Electric?' –
Gary Numan and Tubeway Army

I barely take two steps into the common room at the beginning of our Monday free period when I hear Ella call to me from our usual loitering corner.

'Emily, we need you over here! Georgie needs some advice.'

I make my way over to where the usual gang is assembled, but with a new addition of Georgie. Because Georgie is very tall and serious-looking, we were basically too scared to talk to her between years 7 and 11, at which point Abi was in a school production of *My Fair Lady* in which Georgie played Henry Higgins and Abi learned Georgie was even cooler than we feared, but also extremely kind. Camila and I are avoiding eye contact, and the others have clearly noticed the tension but don't want to take sides, so this Georgie thing provides a welcome distraction for the group.

'Say it all again now Emily's here,' urges Ella.

'OK, so . . .' Georgie begins, as I settle into the only vacant itchy brown common-room armchair in the circle, which happens to be directly opposite Camila, who's still ignoring me.

I'm determined to concentrate on what Georgie's saying, even though my focus has slipped lately, and the low-level buzz of Joe in my brain means I'm permanently distracted. His absence is distracting. The little nuggets of hope are distracting. He's not my friend. He's still just some guy I hardly know. I've been checking my phone so often for a message from him that it's like I'm trying to will one into appearing through sheer persistence, but I've heard nothing since I replied, *Yes, hanging out sounds fun.*

Ugh! I'm meant to be focusing on Georgie!

'. . . I'm dating two people.'

Now she has my attention.

'Tell me more,' I say, leaning in so I don't miss anything.

'Uh, so one is a girl called Sinead, who goes to Our Lady of Lourdes, and the other is Charlie Waters.'

I nod. 'I remember Charlie from reading group one time. What's the problem, then?'

'I don't know . . . the existence of both of them? Simultaneously? They don't know about each other, which I know is bad.' Georgie grimaces. 'I just don't want to have to choose between them.'

I think for a second. 'You know, you might not even have to, right?'

'Do you really think that?'

'I mean, obviously I don't really know how Charlie or Sinead would feel about it, but I think in theory, you don't have to choose. I do think you should bring it up with both of them, though. It might be an uncomfortable conversation about how you don't want to be exclusive, but it's worth having.'

'But you don't think it's, like . . . wrong?' Georgie furrows her brow. I guess she wants to make sure we're on the same page.

'No. Life is long and kind of boring sometimes. One of the best ways to make your time on earth suck less is to surround yourself with cool people. People who make you happy. People who you have fun with. People who make you feel important. And you're super smart and interesting, and you want cool things for yourself, and that kind of narrows down the pool of people who you'll accept into your life, and you've found not one but two lovers that you reckon are good enough for you. That's huge!'

Georgie's smiling. 'I guess you're right.'

'Damn right I'm right. It sounds like *you're* kind of at peace with the situation, but you should still run it by both of them, just to be sure they feel OK about it too.'

'See!' Ella springs back into life after listening patiently to our back and forth. 'I told you she was going to be helpful!'

'Yeah . . . you were right,' Georgie says. 'How do you know all this though, Emily?'

Good question, especially given I've never dated anyone, let alone two people at once.

'I don't really know anything . . .' I trail off, not sure what to say.

'I think you're just good at thinking clearly about stuff,' Abi says.

'Well, you should do whatever you want, Georgie,' Camila pipes up, looking wise and serious, sitting cross-legged on the seat. 'But I could never have an open relationship.'

'You've only been in one relationship for about ten minutes – I don't think anyone's asking you to get yourself another boyfriend as well,' I shoot back. Oops. That's the first thing I've said to her all day. Joe's silence is putting me on edge, and this is what happens.

Everyone's looking down at the floor now.

'Actually,' she thunders back at me, suddenly aflame with righteousness, 'it's been a couple of months, and it's going really well. Thank you for your support.' And with that, she picks up her bag and storms out of the common room.

I regret the comment instantly, mostly because it means I can't maintain my belief that I haven't done anything wrong. Bad Emily.

*

Camila remains absent for the rest of our free period, pushing at my guilt. I copy Abi's physics homework, Ella tests me on my French vocab, and I confirm with the Kendal family that I'm still fine to babysit that evening. Still no Camila.

'Look, I don't know what's going on with you and Camila, but is it really worth all this?' Abi says as we walk to physics.

'No, it's not! It's not at all worth it!' I explode. 'It's like she's got herself a boyfriend and has suddenly become a completely different person.'

'Are you . . .' Abi stops herself and bites her lip.

'Am I what?'

'Are you jealous?'

'Of Ryan?'

'No, not Ryan.' She sighs.

'Then what?'

'Don't be difficult about this, Emily – I'm just asking.'

'Yes, but *what* are you asking?'

'Like, I guess, if you feel somehow betrayed by her because it always used to be you two together, you always had each other, and now she's, like, divided,' Abi says.

'No. She can live her life. I'm happy for her! It's Camila who's getting wound up about this entirely stupid thing that happened before she and Ryan even got together . . .'

Abi gawps at me. 'What the . . . you don't mean the awkward party non-kiss thing with you and him?'

Yes! Thank God! A moment of sanity!

'Yes! That's literally what this is about. That's the whole story! The whole origin of this beef!' I wail, gesticulating wildly with my hands.

'Oh Jesus, maybe you're right. Maybe she has gone mad,' Abi mumbles as we settle down in the lab for an hour of physics fun.

'But it's his fault! He told her about it, and he didn't need to at all. Like, at all. Not one bit,' I hear myself whine.

'Boys are weird, right? Always making trouble where there isn't any . . .'

I turn up to my babysitting job that evening in a terrible mood, which is only lifted when I discover that all Jonah wants to do is read a story and go to bed early (you and me both, buddy), which leaves me a whole evening of paid TV-watching and crisp-eating. I'm halfway through a Kardashian spinoff when my phone lights up on the coffee table in front of me.

Joe

 Are you free on Saturday?

Finally. Finally, he's replied.

# CHAPTER TWELVE

'Take Me to the River' – Talking Heads

Dad looks up as I walk into the kitchen. 'Where are you going looking so nice?'

Just my luck: I knew my run of not-having-to-mention-Joe-to-my-parents would have to end sometime, but I do not want to talk about it today, of all days, the most stressful day. Dad is cleaning the oven while Mum works at the table, glasses on, running her fingers through her short hair. She's nibbling some anaemic-looking crispbread things with Wellness System branding all over them.

'I don't look that nice, do I?' I ask, concerned that it's too apparent I've made an effort (I'm wearing a Breton T-shirt dress with a leather jacket and black ankle boots. I figured it was classic: not too dressy or too *nice* – just right).

Today's the day. Joe has spent the past week recovering from his flu and I suppose has decided that meeting up with me is the best way to return to his social life. I want to dance around with joy. But I don't. Because I'm nervous as hell.

'I don't know how to answer that,' my dad says, looking flustered. 'I'm not sure what I'm meant to say.'

'Yes, where are you off to, treasure?' Mum swoops in, meaning I absolutely cannot avoid the question I'd just dodged successfully.

'I'm going to meet a friend,' I say, but of course by keeping it vague, I've piqued their interest, and they're now keen to know the specifics.

'Which friend?' says Mum, a slight smile threatening to dance across her mouth as she casts a sideways look at my dad, trying to catch his eye.

Are my nerves written all over my face? Can they really sense a shift in my . . . aura, or something?

'Joe,' I mumble.

'Is that with an 'e'?' Dad asks, as casually as possible, not looking up from the sponge he's dragging across the oven.

'I don't know what you hope to learn from whether it's a boy or girl, but if you must know, he's a he,' I reply. This is exactly the kind of conversation that turns me into the archetypal sulky teenager. 'Can I go now?'

'By all means!' says my dad cheerfully, standing up and removing his rubber gloves to hug me goodbye. 'Enjoy yourself!'

***

I keep taking my phone out of my bag, checking to see if Joe has cancelled, but he hasn't yet. He even messaged me last

148

night to confirm our hangout today. I compulsively check for messages as I'm walking to the station. There's one from Abi. I feel guilty that I wish it was from Camila. Still radio silence on that front.

Have fun on your date!

I reply the only way I know how.

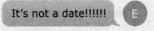

And I mean it. It's really not a date. Even I can accept that. Just because it's not . . . *officially* a date, doesn't mean I'm not looking forward to seeing Joe for a *maybe* date. I shove my phone back in my bag. It's threatening to rain, but I won't let it get me down. Nothing can rain on my parade today.

I try to read my book on the train, but I can't focus. I keep reading the same sentences over and over again. It's been so long since I've seen him that I wonder if I've gone off him. That might be nice. It might be healthy to take a break from being obsessed with him. We've arranged to meet at London Bridge so we can walk along the river to the BFI to see a film later. It's something he likes to do, and I just said yes without looking into it too much.

I gaze out of the window the rest of the way, accepting

that I'm not going to get much out of Margaret Atwood on this train ride. Before I know it, the train is pulling into the station, and I have to transport myself to our meeting point. Oh God, I liked it better when it was up to the train to take me where I needed to go. I click across the station in my boots and try to breathe deeply, but my nerves are threatening to get the better of me. Out of the station, on to the concourse, and down the outdoor escalator by the Shard.

And there he is at the bottom of the escalator. He's looking up at me as I'm gliding slowly down towards him, and I'm desperately trying not to smile. He's just as cute as I remember. Blue is most definitely his colour, and he's looking adorable in a navy-blue plaid shirt and black jeans. Maybe it would be better if I never got to the bottom of the escalator. If I just stayed here forever, always moving towards him but never actually getting there. If I never had to find out what he's really like, never had to get to know him, but could keep him at arm's length and admire him from afar. But I can't, and as I reach the bottom, I'm struck by fear. I realize I don't know what to say to him. What if we have nothing to talk about?

'Hey, Emily,' he says, smiling.

'Hello, Joe,' I reply, not sure if I should go in for a hug. He doesn't, so that's that.

'How have you been?' he asks, as we head towards the river.

'Better than you, I'd guess. Are you all recovered from your lurgy?'

'Yes, I feel loads better. I think I was just in denial that I was so ill, you know? Sorry again that I didn't make it the other night.'

'Look, it's fine. It was a party – it's not like there was no one else there.'

There's an awkward silence for a minute. Oh good, I've run out of things to say already, all my fears have come true, and we haven't even spotted the Thames yet.

'So, is that record player working out for you?'

We press into the mass of people in Borough Market. I want to take his hand so I don't lose him. I wish I was allowed.

'Yes, it's a nice thing to have, but I'm not totally convinced it's much better than listening to music any other way.' I am aware that this is probably an uncool position to take, but it is my position.

'Never tell my dad this, but I agree with you. But . . . it does feel nice to have and to hold, you know?' He's walking slightly ahead of me as we are forced into single file through the throng of people in the market, but he turns back to look at me, and I warm under the glow of his gaze.

151

'I'll keep your secret.' I smile, buoyed at the chance to bond with him.

We break away on to a side street leading away from the main market and are soon down by the river. The clouds have lifted, and it's turned into a pretty nice day for late October. The pedestrian path by the Thames is lively with tourists, buskers, joggers, dog-walkers. We peer over the railing that divides river from land and look at the water. It's a dirty steel colour and lapping gently at the walls. Leaning against the railing together as we look out on to the City on the other side of the river feels romantic, even though it shouldn't. I remind myself silently: this is *not* a date.

'You're right about Arthur Russell, by the way,' Joe says as we continue our stroll up the South Bank.

'What was I right about?' I ask, trying to remember what acute observation I had made.

'That Jens Lekman sometimes sounds like him,' he replies.

'Oh, that. It's nice that you remembered I said that; I forgot . . .' I say. Ugh! Just be cool! Let the chat flow, Emily.

'Well . . . whatever.' He flushes. 'Hey, are you looking forward to the film?'

'Sure I am!' I can't remember what I've said I'll go to see with him; it didn't really seem to matter at the time. I was just chuffed that he wanted to hang out.

'Have you seen *Gentlemen Prefer Blondes* before?' he asks, looking at me expectantly.

'Oh!' I say, before realizing I shouldn't have sounded so surprised. 'Yes, I've actually seen it quite a few times. It's one of my favourites. I watch it with my mum kind of often.' Maybe I shouldn't have admitted that.

'Ah, nice,' he says, but he sounds kind of disappointed, like he wanted to be able to introduce it to me.

We chat easily the rest of the way down the river. We don't run out of things to say to each other, proving yet again that I had nothing to worry about.

It's weird and nice, seeing a film that you've seen a million times before but in a completely new setting, in a new place, with a new person, with new and different feelings. I realize I'm trying to suppress my laughter at bits I think are hilarious but that don't make him laugh, and laughing more than I usually would at the bits he likes. I can even feel myself holding my breath a little whenever something romantic happens, as if willing some kind of transmission to occur between the screen and his brain and my brain.

When the film finishes, he turns to me. 'Do you want to get a drink? It's still kind of early,' he says, looking at his watch.

I don't want him to be thinking about the time. I don't want him to have a point in the future that becomes 'late' that in turn becomes a time at which he has to say goodbye to me.

'Yes, as long as you know somewhere they don't ID,' I say, laughing.

'Oh yeah, I forget about that,' he says. 'You don't seem that young.'

'How old are you, then?' I ask, not sure how to take that comment.

'Nineteen, but only just. It was my birthday last month. OK – let's go and get coffee instead.'

'Many happy belated returns!' I say as he begins to lead us in the direction of the cafe he has in mind. 'Hey, are you still working at Beats Per Minute most of the time?'

'Yeah, although I wish I wasn't. It's kind of a drag. As you know, we don't have that many customers, but my dad seems to think that while I don't have anything "better" to do, it's my duty to put in the hours in the family business,' he says, sounding a little bitter.

'But it seems kind of like a natural home for you, right?' I say. 'You're good at your job.'

It's getting dark now, and I want us to get to where we're going before he decides it's too late, so I walk a tiny bit faster.

'Thanks, but it's not really the job I want to be doing,' he says.

'What do you want to do?' I ask gently.

'I guess I would quite like to be a musician,' he replies quietly.

'That's great! What do you play?' I ask, overwhelmed with a genuine enthusiasm for him pursuing his passion.

'Guitar, bass, and I sing OK,' he says modestly.

'Anyone who says they sing OK clearly sings really well. And hardly anyone can sing really well. So, good for you,' I say, giving him a warm smile.

'I appreciate your belief in me.' He smiles back at me.

Finally, we reach a little cafe the other side of a patch of grass by Waterloo Road. It's small and kind of shabby, and I don't necessarily trust the upholstery. But it's cute, and – more importantly – we're here.

'What can I get you?' Joe asks as we take off our coats and occupy a small table in the far corner.

'Whatever you're having,' I reply smoothly. Smart move: it means I don't have to out myself as someone who almost never drinks coffee.

I can't take my eyes off him while he's ordering. I want to take in every little detail in case this never happens again: his straight back; his hands running through his hair. I want to feel those hands on me, but I can't stop fixating on the memory of Ryan recoiling from me, no matter what he said about Camila being the reason nothing happened.

Joe returns to our table, and I snap out of my daydream.

'Cheers,' he says, and our little glasses of latte clink against each other.

We sip for a moment in silence.

'So . . .' I say, like that isn't the most awkward thing to say when there's an awkward silence.

'So,' he says, looking back at me expectantly.

'What's your music like?' I ask.

'What?'

'The music you make, I mean. What does it sound like?'

'I guess my biggest influence is, like, early Leonard Cohen? But with the . . . expansiveness of Rufus Wainwright. So, kind of acoustic guitars but joyful, you know?' There's a hopeful glint in his eye.

'That sounds really nice,' I say, and I mean it. 'Do you play live, or is it still just your thing?'

'I've been thinking about it. I mean, I can't keep it to myself forever, I guess. It's just very . . . stressful putting yourself out there to be judged by people on something that's so personal and so private,' he says.

Yes, this is the good stuff – tell me about your feelings, Joe.

'That makes a lot of sense,' I say. It does. I wouldn't have the courage to perform in front of people even if I did have any talent. 'Like you say, it can't just be your personal thing forever. Especially if you're serious about it.'

'I think I am,' he says.

'Good for you,' I reply, smiling.

'Oh no,' he says suddenly, looking down at his watch then draining his coffee. 'I have to go. I told someone I would meet them at Waterloo in five minutes.'

'Oh . . . OK . . . Sure . . .' I say, completely taken aback by the abrupt end not only to the conversation about his work, but also to our hangout.

'I'm really sorry. I didn't want to cancel on her, so thought I could do both today. That's OK, isn't it?' he asks plaintively.

'Yes, of course!' I lie, smarting. 'You've got things to do – it's cool.'

'Thanks for being understanding. Hopefully next time we hang out, I won't have to dash off so quickly. If you want to meet up again?'

My heart leaps.

'Of course,' I say. I don't know what else to say.

He pushes open the door to the cafe, and the cold wind hits me. Seems appropriate somehow. I walk with him up to Waterloo so I can take the weird little single-decker bus back along the river to London Bridge. I say goodbye to him outside the Waterloo Road entrance to the station, then cross the road just to get out of the way. I begin to wonder if there really is a pressing engagement this evening, or if he just wanted to get the hell out of there. When I reach the other side of the pedestrian crossing, I look back and see my answer. He's hugging a tall, slim girl with cascading, sleek blonde hair.

Of course. *That's* his kind of girl.

# CHAPTER THIRTEEN

'Blitzkrieg Bop' – Ramones

I do the one thing I know I shouldn't do: I check his Facebook to see if there's any clue as to who the girl was or evidence of where they went. Tap tap tap. A girl called Hannah Neumann checked in with him at the pub opposite Waterloo last night. So that's that, I guess. Whoever you are, Hannah Neumann, I hate you. A lump rises in my throat. But even if my heart is broken, I can't hide here in bed forever. Not least because my mum is committed to rousing me from my snoozing.

'Rise and shine, treasure!' she says as she barges in, opening all the blinds. 'God, you really didn't inherit your father's tidiness gene, did you?'

I must admit, my room is looking particularly bad at the moment: I had to try on various options before I knew I'd found the right outfit for my meet up with Joe yesterday. I shudder internally at the image of me agonizing over different outfits to meet someone who wouldn't have noticed if I turned up in a bin liner. Sweet of me to think my clothes would have made a difference.

'No, Mum,' I groan as I sit up. Mistake! That makes room for my mum to take it as an invitation to come and sit at the foot of my bed.

'So . . .' She smiles coyly, smoothing the wrinkles of my duvet.

'What?'

'How was your date?'

'Mum! It wasn't a date.'

'Of course that's what you would say,' she scolds. 'You never tell me anything about your life!'

'I wish it *was* a date,' I mutter.

'Oh no – what's the matter?' she coos.

'Nothing, Mum. I really don't want to talk about it,' I say, my despair getting the better of me.

'OK, well, I won't push you then.'

Jesus, I must sound miserable if even my mum knows to back off.

'Thank you,' I say sincerely. I squeeze her hand as she gets up to leave my hovel. I'm grateful to her for at least knowing when to stop.

'By the way,' she says from the doorway. 'A letter came from school about university application deadlines. Please don't forget to get your form ready in good time.'

I feel hot with panic. I really do not want to have to make my mind up for definite on this yet, but time is running out.

I'm too wrapped up in the now to think about something that's happening as far away as next year.

Mum changes the subject. 'I'm going to go for a run later – do you want to come with me?'

I can think of nothing I would enjoy less. 'No, that's all right. I'm just going to do some homework today, then go and see Abi's boyfriend's band later,' I reply, propping myself up in bed, as if I'm about to spring into action any minute.

'Are you sure?' she says, looking a bit sulky.

'Yes, I'm sure. When have I ever gone running, anyway?'

'Well, there's no time like the present!' she replies, looking hopeful.

Unfortunately that optimism is misplaced.

'No. Really. I don't want to go. Sorry,' I say, and I hope it sounds final enough to her.

She shakes her head at me in the most patronizing way imaginable but admits defeat.

I thought she had been suspiciously quiet on the diet-and-exercise front recently. It was too much to hope that she had put it out of her mind completely.

I get out of bed and reach for my school bag, trying not to let her words float into my head as I attempt to construct deep and meaningful passages about religion in *Candide*. I wasn't lying when I said I had homework to do. What a bleak Sunday: a day of moping because Joe doesn't fancy me, writing about religious hypocrisy in eighteenth-century France, and fighting off my mother's attempts to turn me into a Healthy Person. Oh, and to top it off, this evening I have to go to the worst pub in town – possibly even in the world.

The Fox stands alone in Croydon. For a town that so prides itself on its campaign against underage drinking, a town that zealously patrols its parks and green spaces to make sure no teenagers are having fun with open containers, a town that would probably ID a pensioner 'just in case', Croydon has truly given up hope with the Fox.

It's not just the floors that are sticky. The walls are sticky too. You don't want to put your stuff down on a surface. It smells like a pint someone's left out in the sun for a thousand years. The toilets are disgusting to the point of being unusable. It's run by a creepy middle-aged man called Colin, who has a dragon tattooed on his face, and who, I suspect, is happy that the Fox is the only place in Croydon underage girls can reliably buy alcohol. The only redeeming feature is that old Colin will let any band play there as long as they can guarantee some attendance. And until I turn eighteen, this majestic shithole is pretty much the only place in my town that I can go out in the evening. I always feel kind of self-conscious when I come here, though. It's all grungy and punky and kind of dirty, and it feels like that look is so much cooler on all the waif-like girls.

Being teenagers, and therefore not a Proper Band, Oliver's lot are on first. Abi sways at the front, flashing encouraging smiles at her man on bass.

'Is it mean if I call them a Poundland Tom Tom Club?' a low voice whispers in my ear.

I'm so surprised that my cider sputters out of my nose.

'Jesus!' I shout, indignant. But of all the people who could sneak up on me, I'm glad that it's Joe. Overjoyed, in fact. 'What are you doing here?'

'I want to support my friend's musical endeavours.' He gestures to the stage.

If I'd known he would be here, I would have made more of an effort. Maybe even gone as far as brushing my hair.

'Even if that involves calling them rip-offs?' I challenge him, with a smile.

'I meant it as a compliment . . .'

Abi elbows me in the ribs for the sin of not paying attention to Oliver's band, but as soon as she sees Joe next to me, her expression changes to pure delight. When Joe turns to go to the bar for drinks, she gestures for me to go after him. Ah, bless Abi. Ruthlessly committed to helping other people follow their dreams.

We don't miss much, as we slip off while the band is playing their last song, but at least it means we beat the rush to the bar. We buy two pints of their cheapest cider and take a seat as far from the stage as is possible in such a cramped space.

'Did you have a nice time last night?' I ask, on the assumption it'll make me look super cool and chilled out if I ask him about his date with the tall blonde lady. I nonchalantly sip at my unrefrigerated draught cider that tastes of urine.

'Yeah, I really did. We just have so much in common. It's so easy to talk.'

'Mmmm,' I nod. What else am I meant to say? Oh, good for you! So glad you've got a dream babe on the go.

'That's why I'm doubly pleased to see you tonight. It was annoying having to run off yesterday,' he says, setting his pint down.

Oh . . . oh . . . he meant me? He thinks *we* have 'so much in common'? He thinks it's easy to talk to *me*? Well I never.

'I'm so sorry about that! I didn't think much of it at the time, but I realized afterwards I didn't even tell you upfront that I would have to dash off, and it probably looked really rude. My mum made me meet my cousin Hannah, who was visiting this weekend. I don't think either of us was particularly bothered, but she was over from Cologne for a flying visit, and you know what mums are like.'

Relief washes over me like a warm shower.

'No, of course – that was no problem at all,' I splutter. OK, so the fact he doesn't fancy me is made slightly more bearable by the knowledge he didn't ditch me last night to meet a girlfriend.

'Do you know the next band?' he asks, craning his head to try to see who's setting up.

'I don't . . . Hey, you should talk to Creepy Colin about playing here sometime. From what you said the other day, I know your stuff is kind of different to this, but they definitely do more chilled nights.'

A smile creeps across his face, but before he can reply, Abi is leaning on the table between us, clearly trying to scope out the situation.

'Emily! Aren't you going to introduce me to your . . . new friend?' she asks, raising her eyebrows to the roof.

I hope she's not going to stay too long, the interlude of quiet between the bands playing is a rare gift.

'Of course. Abi, this is Joe. Joe, this is my friend Abi,' I say stiffly.

'Nice to meet you,' Joe says. 'Although . . .'

'I think maybe we've met before . . .' Abi picks up his thread, waiting to see if he remembers her and is therefore good enough for me.

'Yes, we met outside Beats Per Minute when you were . . . uh . . . hanging out with Oliver,' he says.

'Of course! That must be it . . . Well, I shan't disturb you any longer!'

And with that, she snakes off through the crowd, turning back to blow me a kiss as she goes looking for Oliver. Bless her. She never outstays her welcome. As she goes, I wonder if maybe this is a good tactic: make sure we are surrounded by people who act like we're on a date, and eventually the message will get through to him that we should be on a date. Nice idea.

Joe and I stay at our table while the next band – to whom we have no loyalty but are polite enough to pay attention to – play their set. I keep stealing glances at Joe out of the corner of my eye. His lips just look so kissable. So full and soft and perfect. I honestly think he's the cutest guy I've ever seen. He's definitely cuter than anyone else in the Fox. I wonder if this is how Abi feels about Oliver, or how Camila feels about Ryan, or Ella and Sophia about each other.

I wish we were somewhere quieter. I wish we weren't in the dingiest pub in Croydon. But I suppose I should be grateful that I'm here at all. I came out to make sure there were at least two people in the audience for Oliver's band and was rewarded with a surprise: Joe. Maybe I should do good deeds more often.

After the last band finishes, we stay on and chat for the rest of the evening. An easy back and forth. I laugh a lot, and I'm worried I laugh too much. At least he's funny. And there are worse crimes than laughing loads. I look at him while he speaks and feel a little twist of despair. I want to ask him why he can't just fancy me – just make this easier for everyone and fancy me. I want him to want me. I want him to feel as excited as I do when we meet. I don't just want to be some girl he met at a party who he chats to about music and books and films. I mean, that's not necessarily a bad thing, but it's not the thing I want it to be . . .

Creepy Colin rings the bell to signal last orders, and Joe springs into action, heading up to the bar for our last round. Alone at the table, I catch my reflection in a large mirror hanging behind our seats, and I sit up instantly. I feel hot with embarrassment to have caught my reflection off-guard, slouched in her chair, creating (or, more likely, accentuating) double chins and extra rolls. And the reflection is me, the me that Joe sees when he's talking to me. There's that insistent voice again . . . *You know very well that's why he's not interested in you.* Shut up. Shut up. Shut up.

I'm forced back to reality not by Joe, but by Oliver sliding his lanky frame into Joe's empty seat. I hope he's not planning to stay.

'You played a really good set, Ol,' I say earnestly. I

suppose I can chat to him until Joe gets back from the bar.

'Thanks! I think we're getting better, you know? Maybe not actually *good* yet, but . . . better,' he replies.

Thank God he's not kidding himself he's the next David Bowie.

'Abi tells me you've got a little thing for Joe, right?' he says, looking at me over the top of his thick-rimmed glasses.

I don't know why I would expect her not to say anything to Oliver, but he had better not pass that information along to Joe. The thought of my low-level Joe obsession falling into the wrong hands makes me feel sick with anticipation of the embarrassment and rejection it would mean for me.

'Oh, yeah, that. It's no big deal . . .' I laugh and smooth my frizzy hair to give my hands something to do.

'Well, I would get in there quickly if I were you – he's quite the hot property,' Oliver says.

I'm too confused by what he means to dwell too much on the fact this is probably the longest conversation he and I have ever had.

Oliver nudges me. 'Yeah, from what I know he was pretty popular in his year at Alexander Hall. Lots of female interest . . . Think I even heard whisperings of a threesome or something.'

'Oh. Cool. That's . . . good for him,' I say. What else am

I meant to say? Oh yes please tell me more, Oliver. Tell me all the gory details.

Oliver slaps Joe on the back as he returns to the table, valiantly trying not to spill our drinks.

'Just singing your praises to Em, wasn't I?' he says.

Yes, that's one way to put it.

'I dread to think,' says Joe drily as Oliver gets up and heads off in the direction of Abi.

I spend our last drink sitting bolt upright, shoulders back, my neck elongated to keep my chin up. An attempt at an elegant, ladylike posture. But I'm under no illusions that I look like anything other than a weird robot. Or that it would do anything to help make him find me attractive. Why would it?

We drink up, but I don't want to go anywhere. Not just because there's nowhere else to go in Croydon on a Sunday night. I want to stay here in the warm glow of Joe's attention, even though I know he's not interested. Even though I know he probably has five other girls who he could call right now. Why stop at five? *Ten* girls. I want to keep him close to me, rather than constantly wondering what he's doing, who he's with, where he is. I know that as soon as I'm out of his sight, I'll be out of his mind. If only that was the case for me too.

'It was nice to bump into you tonight,' I say as we make to leave.

'Yes, a very nice surprise,' he replies, buttoning up his coat.

My heart is in my throat: *Come on — just do it.*

'Let's meet up again soon. On purpose.' At least I got the words out of my mouth. Well done, Emily.

'Sure, yes – that sounds good. Let's hang out again,' he says, nodding decisively.

I love the way he keeps using the words 'hang out' just to be extra sure I don't get any wrong ideas about it being a date. Don't worry, Joe: I know it's not a date. I am painfully aware that it is not a date.

'Well, I guess you have my number, so just message me when you feel like it.' I'm trying to cultivate an air of cool. But damn, I hate it when the ball isn't in my court. Oh well, too late now.

'Yes, I do. Great. OK, then,' he says.

Are we meant to hug now? Do we hug? Are we friends yet?

'Wait,' he says suddenly. 'Actually, if you're not doing anything on Thursday evening, why don't you meet me at the shop? Then I can close up, and we can do something after?'

Thursday? That's soon. I was expecting him to delay it at least a couple of weeks. My boldness has paid off, it seems. I take out my phone, pretending to check my calendar.

'Thursday . . . first of November . . .' I mumble faux pensively, feigning surprise to see I am, in fact, engagement free that night. 'All clear! I suppose I'll see you there, then.'

We don't hug – I guess we're not quite there yet – but at least I can head for the bus stop knowing I'll see him again soon. Fortune favours the bold, right?

Now that my next hangout with Joe is officially in the diary, maybe it's time to focus on . . . you know, my actual life. I've been kind of letting it slip lately. I know it's Sunday night, but *boy* do I have that real Sunday-night feeling – like there's something horrible looming ahead of me. I rack my brains and try to think what might be bothering me, but nothing comes.

It's only when I'm sitting at the bus stop, hands jammed in my pockets for warmth, that I notice the poster for the touring production of *Journey's End*, young men in uniform waiting expectantly in a trench. Oh no. Panic rises in me from the soles of my feet to the roots of my hair: that hot, sick feeling; that vertigo; that nightmare grip of fear. I have an essay on First World War poetry due in at 9 a.m. tomorrow. Hours away. Not weeks, not days. Hours. And it's not just any essay; it's my mock A-level coursework. This isn't the sort of thing I *do*! How could I forget the whole thing? I'll tell you how. Joe's pushed everything else out of my head.

Well, that's that. I guess I'll be awake until who knows when. I feel like I'm going to have a heart attack. I nervously tap Morse code on the bus window all the way back to Purley. Pure adrenaline powers me up the hill from the bus stop to my house.

By the time I get home, my parents have already gone to bed. I sneak up to my room as quietly as possible, open my laptop, and throw myself into the trenches. I ignore the clock, disappear into a whirl of words, managing to stay awake through pure fear of not having something to hand in on time. It doesn't matter how long it takes; it just matters that I get it done. It's not my style to just not do essays. Maybe I'll skip revising for the odd test, but not mock coursework. After I don't know how long, I hear a creak on the floorboards outside my room. A slow, tentative knock follows, before my dad's bleary face appears around the doorframe.

'I couldn't sleep, and then I saw your light was on,' he whispers. 'Is everything all right?'

'I messed up, Dad,' I say. Time to confess.

'Why? What did you do?' He looks pained.

'I forgot about an essay. I thought I had more time. I'm an idiot,' I say, exhausted, burying my face in my hands. I hate myself right now for falling so far down this Joe rabbit hole that I just abandoned all my responsibilities. It's amazing how much brain space boys can take up.

'Oh, Emily. You silly sausage.'

'I'm sorry, Dad. I really didn't mean to . . .' I'm trying not to cry. Who cries over homework anyway? 'I know I'm an idiot.'

'You think I never left things till the last minute?' he says kindly.

He's being too kind. But it's what I need right now. Bless him.

'Yeah, but this is, like, last second. And it's a mock coursework essay!' I cry.

He winces, inhales deeply, and sits down on my bed behind me.

'It's not great. There's no two ways about it,' he says. 'And I know it feels important now, but in the long run, you'll see it's no big deal. It's not real coursework; it's not an exam. You're a sensible girl, and I know you won't let it happen again.'

'No, I won't. I really won't.' I really won't. Nothing is worth this stress. I just want to make sure I have some idea of how I'll do in the real thing.'

'Good girl,' he says.

'How are you, Dad? How come you can't sleep?'

'Oh, it just happens sometimes; it's nothing much,' he says breezily. 'But I'm glad I couldn't. I hate the thought of you struggling with this on your own.'

'I'm doing all right, I think. Given the not-ideal

circumstances,' I say. Thank God it's true, bless my past self for at least taking decent notes in class.

'You definitely try harder than your sister ever did. She'd have left it until the last minute on purpose,' he says, smiling.

'What? Katie?' This does not tally with the super-industrious engineering genius I know and love.

'Yes, Katie! As far as I know, you don't have any other sisters.'

'But she works so hard, and she's so good at her job, and she does so well at everything!'

'That only really started when she got to university and was working on stuff she really loved. I don't suppose you were that interested in how much homework your older sister was or wasn't doing – I'm not surprised you don't remember.'

'I thought she'd always been a hard worker.'

'Quite the opposite. It just goes to show that the way things are when you're at school don't always stay that way forever. Or rather, you don't have to stay the way you are forever. Whether that's a good or a bad thing, I don't know. Probably good . . .' He cleans his glasses on his T-shirt. 'It's nice to have time to figure out what sort of person you want to be, what sort of life you want to have.'

'I'm glad to hear things won't be this way forever,' I say, forcing a weak smile through my zombified tiredness.

'Why? What's the matter, treasure?'

'Nothing. I'm fine.'

'Is it . . . boy trouble?' he ventures, raising an eyebrow.

'Yes, but . . . I really don't want to talk about it.'

'That's OK – I'm not going to make you. I just hope it's not worrying you too much.'

'No, it's not,' I lie. I think lying's OK in the pursuit of avoiding an awkward conversation.

'Well, do what you gotta do,' my dad says, before getting up and leaving me to get on with my essay.

I beaver away for another couple of hours and then decide enough is enough. I'm going to bed. I do a final sweep of all my social media and check my emails before turning off my laptop. I think it's my tiredness playing a trick on me when I see a Facebook message notification appear on my phone, and when I click on it, I find it's from Joe.

 **Messenger • 2 min ago** ∨
**Joe**

Hi, Emily! I just wanted to send you this playlist. I felt kind of inspired after the gig and wanted to share with someone who would appreciate it.

There's a link to a Spotify playlist, and even though my eyes are burning from fatigue, my tiredness is outweighed by the lightness in my chest and the butterflies in my stomach. I click the link and am taken to a Spotify playlist full of Talking Heads, Ramones, New Order, right up to Sufjan Stevens and Ryan Adams . . . Except it's the Ryan Adams cover of one of the tracks on Taylor Swift's album *1989*, which made me and all my friends roll our eyes when it came out. I mean, dudes messing with stuff by women and making it worse? Come on!

A twist of irritation niggles, but the warm excitement that he was thinking of me pushes that feeling aside, mingles with exhaustion, and sends me drifting off to sleep.

# CHAPTER FOURTEEN

'True Faith' – New Order

Thursday has come around way too quickly. Dizzyingly fast. I feel sick. I almost don't want to go. I'm so nervous. Arrrrrrgh. I feel like a wild fizzing ball of energy, like my insides are a pinball machine where the stress pings from one side to the other. All my excitement about seeing Joe tonight has converted into pure dread, and I cannot shake it off. Breathe, Emily. Breathe. You're going to have a nice time. This is what you want. You want to get to know him, and you want to spend time with him, so stop trying to talk yourself out of it. Put on your big-girl knickers and be your best charming self. No excuses.

'So . . .' Abi says as she looms over my shoulder while I reapply my pretty, subtle, dusky-rose lipstick.

The lighting in the sixth-form bathrooms leaves much to be desired but, in a crumbling old school like ours, it's certainly not the dingiest corner I could have found. I wish Camila was here, gently reassuring me. Instead I have to make do with Abi's boundless, energetic optimism. Camila is still stewing in her righteous indignation. Maybe energetic optimism is actually what I need right now?

'How are you feeling?'

'I feel fine. Honestly!' Not honestly at all. In fact, very dishonestly. I want to vomit. I keep thinking about what Oliver said to me on Sunday night, about how many girls are presumably chasing after Joe. I don't stand a chance.

'Are you excited?' Abi dances around me, twisting her streamlined hips and waist in an approximation of a sexy grind.

Excited is maybe half of what I'm feeling. The other half is some sort of mix of scared, anxious and deeply, deeply curious as to how this will play out. There are so many potential outcomes, and I'm nervous to find out what will actually happen. But yes, I am excited.

'Yes,' I say decisively, clicking the lid back on to the tube of lipstick and shoving it in my bag. 'Yes, I am excited.'

'What are you going to do? Where are you going to go?'

'I don't know the answer to either of those questions. All I know is I'm meeting him at Beats Per Minute, and then we'll figure it out from there. You know, it's just . . . casual.'

I'm trying to sound chilled out rather than terrified. The vagueness of the plan concerns me, as if it might not be real, or it might be easy for him to back out of. But I try to push those thoughts out of my mind and just look forward to seeing him. I try to conjure up a vision in my mind of pom-pom-wielding cheerleaders surrounded by fireworks spelling out 'T-H-I-N-K P-O-S-I-T-I-V-E, E-M-I-L-Y!' I suppose Abi isn't such a bad cheerleader herself.

'I know you say that, but this one feels like a proper date, you know?' She squeals, with a feverish excitement that I can't match.

Just as I open my mouth to protest, a cubicle door bangs open, and who should emerge but Horrible Holly.

'You've got a date? Really? How precious.'

I sigh. 'No, I don't.' Congrats, fate, on finding me the only person that could make me feel even more nervous before seeing Joe and throwing them into my path. Real cool. 'I'm just meeting a friend.'

'That sounds more likely,' she replies, smirking to herself as she takes an inordinate amount of time to wash her hands at the sink next to us.

'What's that supposed to mean?' Abi snaps, defensively.

Even though I know she means well, I have to suppress an instant groan. I wish she hadn't bothered.

'Oh nothing, I just didn't know the fuller figure was back in fashion.'

I feel all my nervous energy build up inside and turn into a boiling rage with nowhere to go. I feel my face flush with embarrassment and anger that it always comes back to this, and there's nothing I can do about it.

'You know what, Holly?' I say as she's drying her hands on some paper towels. 'Screw you.' And I do something I've never done before. I push her. Not hard. Not *into* anything. But I do push her. And the sensation of relief I feel as my hands make contact with her shoulders is like squeezing a spot or something. I know it's wrong, but it feels so right – and in that moment, it's so satisfying.

She gasps but rights herself, then stares at me, lip curled. 'All right, then,' she says. 'I see how it is.' She barges out of the toilets, looking haughty and aggrieved.

'Holy . . .' Abi trails off and gapes at me in complete disbelief.

'What, like she didn't have much worse coming for a really long time?'

'No, totally,' says Abi. 'I just didn't ever think it would be you that cracked. You, the one that doesn't care about what people think.'

I brush my hair in silence while Abi eyes me with apparent newfound respect. It's not the worst reputation to have: someone who 'doesn't care about what people think'. But it's more pressure, isn't it? Pressure to keep not caring. And when you do care, it becomes a huge deal.

'Um, anyway, have you done your UCAS form?' I ask, changing the subject. I'm hoping she'll say no.

'Yes, I sent it off last week – couldn't miss that Cambridge deadline,' she replies.

This half makes me feel better, because I don't want to go to Cambridge, but it also troubles me because the fact remains that, all around me, people are making their minds up about what they're going to do with themselves – and I'm not.

Leaving the girls' loos, Abi and I trudge down the long, winding staircase of the sixth-form block. Part of me doesn't want to get to the bottom. But of course we do, and before we know it, we're out in the cold November dusk. Darkness has started to fall surprisingly quickly lately, and since I spent so long loitering in the bathroom, attempting to beautify myself for Joe, it already feels like evening. Abi walks me up past McDonald's, past the weird army surplus store that's definitely run by a neo-Nazi, past the charity shops, and leaves me at the corner of the side street where Beats Per Minute has its home.

'Goodluckhavefun,' she says all in one breath so it becomes one word, our go-to mantra, benediction, whatever you want to call it. She pulls me into a bear hug. 'You're going to have a great time. Don't worry so much.'

I try to take her words to heart.

As I round the corner and Beats Per Minute looms into view, I feel moved by the vibrant blue of the shopfront. There's hardly anything else on this street. No one cares about it at all. And you probably wouldn't even come down here unless you were looking for the shop. But Joe's family care enough to keep their corner of the world looking beautiful. The thought calms me as I push the door, but it doesn't move. I start to panic. Have I got the wrong day? What the hell? I scrabble around in my bag for my phone. No message from Joe. My head snaps up as I hear a *clunk-click* in front of me, and there's Joe unlocking the door from the inside. A smile spreads across my face, and I hope against hope he can't read the relief in my expression that he turned up at all.

'Hello, you,' he says with a grin, ushering me into the shop.

What's up with that phrase, huh? Even when it's used in an entirely neutral, friendly way, it sounds like flirting.

'Hi! Are you all done for the day?' I ask as I set down my jacket on top of the New Releases section.

'Yes. As you can guess from the locked door, we're not expecting any more customers,' he replies, to my great relief. 'I've put in an honest day's work and can now hang out with you guilt free.'

'More than I can say for myself.' This is true. I did not put in an honest day's work at school. Also, I physically assaulted someone. Guilt free, I am not. 'Hey, what do you want to do tonight?'

'Well, there's nothing much going on anywhere . . . and I don't really want to go to the Fox again,' he says.

Oh no – what does this mean for me? Am I going to have to suggest something? Is he going to abandon me and our hangout altogether?

He shrugs. 'So, I was thinking maybe we could just hang out here.'

'Oh!' I chirp. 'That sounds nice.' It does sound nice. More than anything, I just want to chat to him with no distractions, no one ringing a bell for last orders, no one rushing us out of the restaurant because they need the table back.

'Also, I just bought a new guitar, so I have, like, *no* money.' He smiles sheepishly.

Oh, OK – so that's his angle. Not, *Oh – wouldn't it be nice to spend some proper time alone with Emily, that super cool and cute girl.* Of course not.

'Yeah, that's cool. I get it,' I say. Chilled out. That's me. Famously relaxed.

He rounds the counter and dips out of sight for a second before reappearing with a bottle of wine and two glasses. OK, could be worse. He leads me up a set of stairs that are blocked off to the public, up to a mezzanine level that overlooks the shop floor. There just isn't enough stock or customers, he explains, to justify it being open upstairs any more. Plus, he adds bitterly, it made it too easy for people to nick stuff when they were out of sight up here. Now his family just uses it as a place to keep their junk: cardboard boxes, rolls of tape, marker pens.

We're standing on a worn-through patterned rug, which covers the floorboards in the centre of the mezzanine, around which are scattered a few sagging beanbags. Joe nods in their direction.

'I like having somewhere out of the house that I can come to read or play guitar without anyone bothering me,' he explains. 'Anyway, I was going to put on some music. Is there anything you want to hear? You'll never be in a better place to have your musical whims satisfied,' he says, gesturing around the shop.

'The one thing I always want to listen to whenever I get the chance is 'Why' by Carly Simon,' I say, poised to give an explanation for why this so readily tripped off my tongue. I wonder if I should have pretended to give it more thought.

'Yeah, it's an absolute classic.'

No explanation needed.

'I was thinking something more sedate, but I would be a bad shop assistant if I wasn't catering to your needs. The customer is always right.'

'Who needs sedate when you can have an absolute

banger, though?' I'm very committed to this song, and he will not deter me.

Joe dashes downstairs and reappears moments later with my record of choice, plus another tucked under his arm. I can tell from the washed-out yellow and brown tones of the cover that it's *Songs of Leonard Cohen*. Of course he would like that; I like that. He blows the dust off the case of a record player that is sitting on a desk in the corner of the mezzanine and sets up the record, gently dropping the needle in place. The machine leaps into action, and the shop fills with the sound of that bouncing, distinctly eighties faux-reggae beat overlaid with Carly Simon's mournful vocals.

We sit cross-legged on the beanbags as he pours the wine. As we drink, the song eventually fades out, and Joe leaps to his feet to change the record.

'This is just something I like listening to at this time of year,' he says, blushing as the first track, 'Suzanne', starts up, the soft, low scratch of the vocals lapping against the restless guitar like a wave.

'Um, that's OK . . . You don't have to explain yourself to me. I would be surprised if someone had heard this record and didn't love it. It's a nice choice.'

And then a question occurs to me. 'Where . . . did you come from?'

'What?' He lowers his glass and looks at me with a furrowed brow.

'I mean, I'd never seen you before Ben's party at the end of August.' I sure as hell would have remembered if I'd seen him around before then, I think (but don't say). 'How did you end up there?'

'Oh, well, I kind of flunked my A levels,' he says, shifting uncomfortably on his beanbag. 'So I didn't get into the uni I wanted to go to. So I'm kind of stuck here for a while, and I figured all my friends are going to uni this year, so I'll need some new parties to go to. Oliver comes in here sometimes, so he invited me, and I thought, why not.'

So if he hadn't messed up his A levels, he would be somewhere else right now. And I would have no idea who he was.

'I'm sorry that happened . . .' I say. But I'm not really.

'It's OK. I'm retaking some stuff in January, and that should sort me out for next year. It was just kind of a shock at the time.'

'Was it . . . for any particular reason? Or did it just happen that way?'

'Well, my parents separated, ahead of getting divorced. Which I didn't really see coming. Or rather, I had always kind of ignored the signs that it was on the cards. I thought they argued a normal amount, and I thought they disliked each other a normal amount, I guess. And the whole thing was just . . . extremely distracting.'

'But they still run the shop together, right?'

'They still run the shop *separately*, but together. They haven't figured out what to do with it yet. You'll never catch them in here at the same time. I'm their little go-between: I pass on messages and deal with stuff for them. At least for the time being.'

'I'm really sorry. That must be hard . . . being in the middle.'

He smiles. 'Yeah, it is.'

Following a tense silence, I offer up a worry of my own. 'I'm really dragging my heels with university applications. I know I want to go, I know I probably want to do English, but part of me feels like I should go somewhere far, far away to, like, assert my independence or something. Like my sister, who's living a whole new life in Manchester and is loving it.'

'And the other part of you?'

'Knows I want to be in London. It's familiar and scary at the same time. Like, it's a place I know quite well because I go there a lot since we live so close, but it's also a place I've never lived in, and I want to find out what that's like. But there's this pressure to go out and explore and kind of embed yourself in a new world, but . . . I think I need some level of comfort and familiarity.' I suddenly realize what those words really mean to me. 'I need to feel like I could see my family easily if I wanted to.'

'You know, all of those are really good reasons,' he says gently. 'So, you get on with your parents? Are they still together?'

'They are, and I do. Well, sort of. My dad is great because he's so calm and creative and thoughtful, but it can be kind of difficult with my mum.'

'Yeah?'

'Yeah,' I say, wondering how much detail to go into. 'She makes our relationship difficult because it feels like she wants to change . . . *things* about me. Which I'm kind of not that bothered about changing. But anyway. I try to spend time with her when I can because . . . I've only got one mum, I guess. She tries, even though it's in the wrong way.'

'I get you.'

'I just feel like a baby, wanting to be close to them. Like I should have grown out of it or something. It's not like I would want to see them every day, just . . .'

'Knowing that you could if you wanted to?' Joe says.

'Yeah. That,' I say.

'I think you know what you're doing. It doesn't matter what everyone else is doing or what they think you should do.

You know *you* better than anyone. You've got to trust your instincts.'

We sit for a moment before I prod the conversation towards music and bands, and from there, we have nothing to worry about. It's a smooth back and forth between us as we hop from Nile Rodgers' production to sixties girl groups to the greatest cover versions of all time.

'Um, are you OK?' he asks suddenly, glancing over his shoulder at me as he turns the record over. 'You look kind of . . . pale. Dizzy.'

'Yeah, I'm fine,' I say, as 'So Long, Marianne' starts up.

'Look, let's just skip the booze – it's a school night anyway. There's some orange juice downstairs. Just a sec, I'll go and get it.'

Sweet relief. I know it sounds pathetic, but I can't think of anything better than warm orange juice with Joe.

He creaks back up the stairs, and I notice it's started to rain outside. Even from the back of the shop, we can hear the dull, persistent thud of fat raindrops against the window. Joe flicks on a heater.

'Yeah, it's not so cosy in here sometimes,' he says.

'No, I like it. Your little corner of the world. It's a good place to be,' I reply.

He smiles. I melt. The way his cute nose turns up at the end when he grins. The way his eyes twinkle behind his glasses. We hold each other's gaze for a bit too long, and my heart fills up. It feels like I'm listening to 'Maple Leaves' off the album I bought from him. All swoonsome and dreamy—

'*Aaaachoo!*' I erupt in a sneeze. The dust has got the better of me. Great timing. It's so loud that Joe laughs.

As I'm rummaging in my bag for a tissue, I lay various things out on the floor. My notebook, my small make-up bag, my copy of *What I Loved*. Joe picks it up and turns it over in his hands.

'Siri Hustvedt, huh? Isn't that Paul Auster's wife?'

'Sure is, my friend.' I was going to ask if he's read it, but . . . clearly not.

'Have you read anything by him?' He tosses the book back to me without another glance, and I stuff it back into my bag.

'No, not yet. But I'm loving this book. Really, really loving it. It's making me want to go to New York and look at art—'

'Wait, you haven't read anything by Paul Auster?' he interrupts me, sounding not at all interested in hearing about *What I Loved*.

Like the sound of a glass shattering, something dawns on me. 'Do you know you never recommend things by women when we talk about books or music or films or TV or whatever?

Do you consume any media by women? Like, ever?'

He sighs. 'Stuff isn't automatically good just because it's by women, you know.'

'First, yes I do know. Second, way to avoid answering my question.'

He sighs. 'Yes, I do "consume media" by women,' he says, defensively punctuating his words with air quotes.

'OK, fine, whatever – I'm sure you're right,' I say, sensing that the shift in mood has brought the evening to an end. I feel like I've run out of steam. And I don't want to overstay my welcome. The thought of him waiting for me to leave is too cringe to bear. 'It's getting late. I think I'm going to head off.'

'Oh, are you sure?' Joe asks, surprised. 'I can walk you to the bus stop if you want?'

'No, that's OK. I'm sure I can make it on my own,' I say, getting up and throwing my bag over my shoulder.

We descend the rickety stairs in silence. While I'm putting on my jacket at the door, I try to brush off the weirdness that just passed between us and strike up conversation again.

'Thanks for having me,' I say. Even if he can be a bit defensive, I guess there's still nowhere else I'd rather have been tonight.

'It's no problem at all,' he says.

He looks like he's about to give me a hug goodbye when his eyes seem to illuminate with an idea or a memory. He paces over to the till.

'Before you go, I wanted to give you this,' he says, fumbling under the counter and producing – what else – a record.

I gasp with delight: the new album by my beloved fat feminist icon Lee Klein and her band the Hairpins. Lee's face dominates the sleeve, contorted into a wild scream. Her chin pressed against her neck making it impossible to conceal the fullness of her face. 'NO BIG DEAL' is printed over her mouth in neon-pink spray paint.

'Oh . . . wow . . .' I'm taken aback. I would have been fine streaming this on my phone. But to have it, to really *have* it physically, and for it to be a gift from Joe.

'We didn't get many in, and we're probably not going to sell many. You know, to the middle-aged man contingent of Croydon's record-buying public. I thought at least one copy would be better off with you.'

'That's really kind of you. Thank you so much. I feel like I haven't even mentioned that I like the Hairpins, let alone love them,' I say, overwhelmed with gratitude.

'I just took a chance, I guess,' he says. 'She seems like your kind of girl.'

'Have you listened to it?' I ask.

'I haven't. But I will if you tell me it's good.'

There's something about that which makes me glow a little inside. It wrestles with my insecurities. Maybe it'll even win.

# CHAPTER FIFTEEN

'Here You Come Again' – Dolly Parton

The next morning, I decide to walk to school to clear my head. I'll put something fun like *Stop Making Sense* by Talking Heads on my headphones, and I'll stomp all the way there.

I'm barely down the hill to the main road when I feel the insistent *buzz-buzz-buzz* of my phone in my pocket. Who calls people in this day and age? I wriggle the phone out of my jeans pocket and check the screen. Katie.

'Hi, Katie.'

'Hello, baby sausage. How are you?'

'I'm all right – just communing with nature by walking to school.'

'I can hear the traffic from here. There ain't much nature on the main road between home and school, pal.'

'OK – "communing with nature" was maybe a bit extreme. I just wanted some time on my own. Anyway, what is the purpose of your call?'

'I just thought I'd give you a ring before school while I knew you wouldn't be busy. I realized I hadn't spoken to you in ages. Every time I call the house to speak to Mum and Dad, you're out. You seem to be out all the time these days, which I entirely approve of.' I can hear the smile in her voice. 'Why so busy these days? Have you got a boyfriend? Or a girlfriend? I mean, either's fine. Or both. Or neither.'

'I don't have a boyfriend . . .' I trail off. 'But there is someone I like. A lot.'

'Oh, how fun! Is it going well? Are you happy?'

'No to all of the above,' I say morosely.

'Do you want to tell me about it?'

'Maybe. I don't know. I kind of hate talking about it because talking about it only proves to me that I really care about it, and I don't want to care, because caring is painful.'

'I can try to give you my best non-patronizing adult advice. Or at least, I promise I won't judge you.'

I pause for a moment, hesitant to open up. But then I think about it. There are worse people to confide in than my older sister. So I launch into a detailed explanation of Joe: who he is, how I feel about him, and everything that happened that took us up to last night. Katie doesn't interrupt my flow, and makes all the right listening noises, only interjecting with useful questions where appropriate.

'OK, so last night sounds like it was weird, right?' I say once I've finished filling her in. 'Like it was all going super well, all cosy and nice and records and beanbags and rain against the window, then all of a sudden, it wasn't, and then before I could run off, he gives me the new record by my favourite band. But I don't know how to feel about it. Overall good? Overall bad? Both? Neither?'

'Well, obviously I can't say either way because I'm not you, and I wasn't there – but it does sound like this hangout last night was . . . I guess, weirdly stressful, because it sounds like you never really know where you stand with him,' she says.

'Yes! That's the problem: I can never tell if he just wants to hang out as a friend or if he might be interested in me . . . like *that*. But we have a great time when we do hang out.'

'To be honest, he wouldn't spend so much time with you if he didn't want to. I can't know for sure the nature of his feelings for you, but I don't think he'd hang out with you if he didn't like you.'

'That's the thing. I know he likes me, because I'm obviously extremely cool as I'm sure you would agree,' I say, leaving a beat for Katie to confirm, which she grudgingly does. 'But what I don't know is if he *likes me* likes me. Like, does he fancy me?' I feel ridiculous saying this out loud, but it really is the only question I want an answer to right now.

'I wish I could give you the answer, but even in my infinite wisdom, I cannot. But this isn't like you, matey – you're not usually stressed out like this. Maybe that's not a good sign?'

'I guess it's because he's all super-experienced, which intimidates me and makes me feel like an idiotic baby? I mean, to begin with, I thought he was just a regular guy, but it turns out he's some kind of super-stud, having sex with a thousand girls (give or take).'

'You can't do anything about how much sex someone has or hasn't had. And more than that, it's kind of irrelevant to what sort of person they are. I guess all you can judge him on is his actions towards *you*,' she says.

'You're right. You're right – I know you're right,' I say, quoting our favourite film, *When Harry Met Sally*. It's something Katie and I say to each other when what we really want to say is, 'I know what you're saying is true, but I don't care, and I'm going to keep doing the opposite thing anyway.'

'Trust me. Who he's had sex with is not the important piece of this puzzle. I think you getting so stressed and tangled in this is more important. But what do I know.'

'You know a lot,' I say.

'OK, little one – I'm at work now, so I have to go, but I'm really happy you opened up to me about this, and I hope I said at least one helpful thing.'

'You did. You're great. I love you,' I say. I'm not used to speaking this openly to anyone, even my sister. But the distance and the phone make it feel easier to talk.

As I hang up, I realize, against all odds, I feel calmer about Joe. I feel like I'm a part of his life now. Maybe I'd even go as far as to say he feels like a new friend. I don't feel like he's just going to disappear into the ether any more, that one unanswered message means I'll never see him again. Since 'absence makes the heart grow fonder', maybe the reverse is also true, and presence makes the heart grow . . . less fond? Maybe seeing him more, having him around, is good for keeping a lid on my feelings. And it's important for me to know that. To realize that I can stand up for things I think are important, even when it means disagreeing with a really, really cute guy – and I don't have to panic when it happens.

Although hanging out with Joe last night made it feel like a Friday, unfortunately it wasn't, and I still have to sit through a whole day of school today. But for the first time in weeks, I listen, properly, all the way through physics and French and English. I feel secure in myself, in what I'm doing. I don't have to peer over anyone's shoulder at their notes to find out what my teacher just said. I say smart things in class, rather than zoning out and retreating into my thoughts. Talking to my sister has cleared my head better than any solo walk could have done. School's not so bad this year, and I don't have much of it left.

\*

It's been a good day. I descend the stairs from the sixth-form block slowly at 3.45 p.m., content that it's the weekend, content that everything seems roughly in good order. I hear someone skittering down the stairs at high speed behind me and only realize it's Holly when she makes a point of overtaking me. Oh God, Holly. For all the highs and lows of Joe, I'd forgotten about my run-in with her. I'll bet you anything that she hasn't forgotten. She stands at the bottom of the stairs, holding the door open and looking up at me as I cautiously pick my way down the last set.

'Come on, slowcoach,' she says cheerily.

What is this, a PE lesson? Any excuse to rub it in.

'I'll hold the door for you as long as you promise not to beat me up again.'

'All right, all right, all right,' I say. 'I'm coming. And . . . I'm sorry about what happened the other day.' I'm not really sorry, but if she's willing to brush it off, then it's better for everyone if I do too.

'Oh, that's OK,' Holly says absent-mindedly, not looking at me, instead scanning the street outside. 'Who's he?' she asks, peering around the door, raising her eyebrows and cocking her head.

'Who's who?' I ask, rounding the door that Holly's propping open. 'Oh!'

My heart speeds up in seconds. He's there. He's right

there. Well, Joe certainly gets Holly's seal of approval. Her eyes are practically sticking out on stalks like in a cartoon.

'That guy with the green sweatshirt,' she says. 'Ohmygod – is he waving at you?'

'Yeah . . . he's . . . my friend, I guess,' I say. What else am I meant to say? He *is* my friend.

Holly eyes me with a look of respect I haven't seen in her before. Yeah, Holly – you underestimate me. I'm not just a tragic fat loser. I'm a cool fat babe. With attractive male friends.

'Well . . . have fun with your mate,' she says, dismissing me with a screwface and a patronizing wave.

Clearly her respect was never going to last long.


'Friend of yours?' Joe asks, shouldering his backpack as we start walking.

'Absolutely not,' I reply. 'Entirely not.'

What's with his new habit of turning up in unexpected places? Is he doing this to mess with me? First, he disappears for weeks – at the peak of my crush, he was nowhere – and now it feels like he's everywhere.

'Not at work today?' I ask, as casually as humanly possible. Of course he's not at work; he's right here.

'No, my mum's holding down the fort today,' he replies.

We walk on in silence. Why is he here? Is it rude to ask why he's here?

'Hey,' he says, as we turn the corner and start the gentle slope up to the centre of town. 'You left in kind of a rush last night. I just wanted to make sure you were OK.'

'Me? Yes, I'm fine. I'm really good, actually. I feel better about things than I have for a long time,' I say, beginning to relax about his unexpected appearance.

'Tell me about it?' he says. 'Tell me about the things you feel good about.'

So, without telling him how much his appearance in my life threw me off-course, I tell him about getting my focus back. I tell him about messing up and forgetting to do my essay. I tell him about everything great I've listened to lately. I tell him that even though I'm not entirely sure what I'm going to do next year, I'm fairly confident I'll make the right choice. And we walk. And we walk. And we walk. We walk in circles, we double back on ourselves, we just keep going and we can't stop. We walk past the town hall, past the alley where reggae music is always playing, past the cinema, past the shopping centres, through the shopping centres, down to West Croydon, up to East Croydon. The ground is slick with rain, but the sky has cleared, and it's a beautiful, crisp evening, and there's no one I would rather be here with. The atmosphere seems to crackle and fizz with possibilities. It feels like we both know our aimless walking will have to come to an end at some point, but

I desperately don't want it to. I told my dad I'd be in for dinner. It's dark already.

I mime looking at my watch, because it was only when I looked down at my wrist to check the time that I remembered I don't actually wear one. 'Well, I should get back home,' I say.

'Oh, of course.'

Does he sound slightly disappointed? We're only a couple of streets away from my bus stop. All the possibilities are now contained within these two streets. But conversation has dried up. I've broken the spell. We can't pick the threads back up now. We walk on in silence until we reach the bus stop.

We stand facing each other – my heart is beating so hard that it feels like it's going to burst out of my chest. I want to wrap my arms around him and kiss him and kiss him so I can find out what it feels like to be that close to him. Joe breathes deeply and fixes me with a serious look. Oh my God, can he read my thoughts? Does he know I'm thinking about how much I want to kiss him?

'I've been thinking about what you said last night about media by women. Maybe you're right. Do you reckon you could make me a playlist to show me what I'm missing?' he says.

I blush. I feel light-headed. 'Huh, that was a quick turnaround,' I say.

'Yeah, yeah, I know,' he says, scratching his head and smiling that completely devastating smile of his. 'It was just hard to be put on the spot like that.'

'Well . . . thank you for thinking about it, I guess,' I reply. 'And, sure, playlists are kind of my speciality, so I'll see what I can do.'

I look over his shoulder at the bus timer countdown. Its orange LED display tells me it's coming in one minute. I don't ever want it to appear. But there are no excuses any more, no reason to prolong the evening. We've had a good run. As a bus rounds the corner, my heart sinks . . . but it's not my bus! I still have time! Time for what? What do I want? The first bus, the not-my-bus, pulls away, and behind it, hulking into view, is mine. Game over. I stick my arm out so it'll stop.

'I had a really good time,' I say as the bus pulls up next to me.

'Me too. I'm glad I waited outside your school like a weird creep,' he says, chuckling.

The sexiest weird creep there ever was.

'You can be a weird creep any time,' I reply.

Everyone else has got on the bus.

'You'd better go! Buses wait for no man. Or girl,' Joe says, drawing me in for a hug.

And what happens next is something that I can only describe as feeling like an out-of-body experience. I look him in the eye for a second as we pull apart, and in that split second, my brain and my body separate. I kiss him. On the lips. When we separate, his mouth has formed a tiny 'o' of shock. He says nothing.

I hop on to the bus just before the doors close, and it pulls away mercifully quickly.

I dare to take a backwards look out of the window as we're driving away, and Joe's still there, just standing motionless at the bus stop. Oh my God! What have I done? Everything was going so well – why would I do that? No, wait, I did that *because* everything was going so well. I was lured into a false sense of security. Oh God, how unbelievably embarrassing. I don't do things like that. And I don't do things like that for a good reason – they just don't turn out well! Why would this time be any different at all? I feel hot all over. Who wants to get pounced on in public by a fat girl?

I check my phone. No message. Why would he have messaged me? Oh no, is this going to be the beginning of some interminable waiting process where I spend the next week checking my phone for a message to clear the air, and the message never comes, and eventually I just go mad instead? Why did I open this particular can of worms? Why couldn't I just be grateful for what I had?

I can't get comfortable in my seat on the bus; I can feel the divide between my seat and the one next to me pressing into the bottom of my thigh. I catch myself reflected in the dark window pane and wish I could shrink myself down from this great, hulking mess of a person to someone dainty and dignified. Someone loveable. I try to sit up, try to give myself a little help with my posture, but it's no good. Nothing so minor could help me. I'm beyond help. Joe's arms had to go so far to reach around me, no wonder he was surprised when I kissed him.

I need backup.

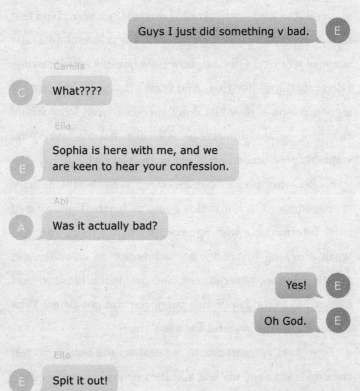

Guys I just did something v bad.

Camila

What????

Ella

Sophia is here with me, and we are keen to hear your confession.

Abi

Was it actually bad?

Yes!

Oh God.

Ella

Spit it out!

I . . .

Ella

THIS IS SOPHIA ON ELLA'S PHONE.
WE DEMAND TO HEAR WHAT U DID.

I just kissed Joe . . .

Abi

Camila

Why is that bad?

Ella

Yeah, we are struggling
to see the bad part here.

Because I kissed HIM,
not the other way around!

Abi

So??? Get what u want.

Camila

You're cool and confident –
why would u wait for him?

So I could be sure! Now I'm just,
like . . . does he like me? Did he want
me to do that? Is he horrified???

Abi

What happened after the kiss?
What did he say?

Nothing! My bus came. He just stared
at me and didn't say A N Y T H I N G.

Camila

I'm proud of you. I could never
be confident enough to do that.

Noooo – you're meant to tell me that's
exactly what you would have done too.
God, this was such a mistake, I hate
myself. Now I just have to wait and see
if he ever speaks to me again. I feel like
such a CREEP.

Ella

You're not a creep, matey. You just took
matters into your own hands. I applaud u 👏

I'm just going to try to put the
whole thing out of my mind . . .

Abi

If that makes you feel better, then do it.

Camila

Do you want me to come
over and therapize you?

C

If you're not doing anything • • E

Camila

C    I'll come over after dinner xxxx

Abi

Don't get too down over this.
A    I reckon u did a good thing.

Ella

E    Us too. Stay strong etc.

The fact that Camila has finally decided to break the ice between us is all that gets me through the bus ride home without crying.

'Nice of you to join us,' my dad calls cheerily from the kitchen as I push the door closed.

At least I'm still in time for dinner.

'Sorry – I just met a friend after school,' I say, hanging up my coat and slumping into a seat at the kitchen table.

'I've made pork belly for dinner. Of course, Mum is having something else . . .'

'Oh no, she's not still on her Wellness thing is she?' I groan.

'I think so, but this is something else – something about blood type. I've stopped asking,' he says, shaking his head.

Mum carries in a plate of raw vegetables. Bleak. I try to put Joe out of my mind while we eat, but that image of his shocked face and the feeling of a hard, unready mouth against mine keep floating back to me like a bad dream. I feel dizzy with embarrassment as I eat, barely tasting the food.

'Earth to Emily?' Dad's voice floats to me as I'm replaying the scene yet again.

'Oh, sorry, Dad. I was a million miles away.' Actually, only about one mile away and one hour ago, but still . . . very much not here.

'I was asking if you wanted any more pork; I made too much,' he says, casting a glance at Mum as he heads for the kitchen.

'Sure, why not,' I say noncommittally.

'Or you could have some of this?' Mum gestures at the raw vegetables on her plate.

'It barely looks like enough for you, let alone me as well.'

'It's more than enough for me,' she replies tersely. 'We eat far more food than we need to as a culture.' She looks haughty and superior, like she's secure in the knowledge that she's unlocked the secret to eternal life.

'Have you ever considered that your bad mood might

be caused by the fact you're permanently malnourished?' I say, deliberately dropping my knife and fork from a height so they clatter on to the plate. 'Maybe if you ate more normally, you'd be able to have a conversation with people about something other than food.'

Before anyone has a chance to speak, the doorbell rings. Saved by the bell.

'Camila's here – I should answer it,' I say, plodding off to the front door. The relief of seeing her standing there is immense.

In that moment, I know that we're back to normal.

'Thank you for coming,' I say as I flop on to my bed with a huge sigh.

'That's OK – you seemed stressed . . .' Camila smiles gently. 'And I'm kind of bored of avoiding you, you know?' she says, sitting down on the floor.

'I'm really, really, extremely glad to hear that.'

'I know I overreacted. You don't have to tell me.'

'OK. I won't,' I say as a warm feeling spreads through me. I can't help smiling. 'I'm not a threat to your relationship, I promise.'

'I know – it's irrational of me. Just hearing that Ryan liked you made me feel so scared of losing him. It's so stupid, and I wanted to be better than that, but I'm clearly not,' she says, biting her lip and stroking the pile of the carpet one way and then back the other like you would a cat. 'I feel so bad for taking it out on you; it was just so stupid of me. I guess getting a boyfriend has made me go a bit mad.'

'Uncharted territory, innit.'

She shrugs. 'I'm really sorry.'

We sit in silence for a moment, just happy to be together. Happy to not be nursing a stupid, pointless grudge.

'So, is having a boyfriend totally amazing?' I finally ask.

Camila instantly lights up. 'Kind of, yeah. It's just nice having someone who you know is always on your team, you know? Like someone who's meant to care specifically about *you*,' she says. 'Someone who makes you feel good.'

'Does he make you feel good, then?'

'Having a boyfriend makes me feel good,' she says, blushing and flicking a glance at me as though anxiously anticipating my reaction.

'I'm glad,' I say, slightly stiffly. 'Do you think that you getting a boyfriend has anything to do with . . . you know . . .' I can't bring myself to spell it out, but I don't have to.

Camila blushes again and lowers her eyes. 'I don't, actually,' she says, shrugging. 'He said he'd been thinking about asking me out all summer while I was away. I don't think it has anything to do with it. It's just a thing that happened.'

'Oh yeah, I kind of . . . keep forgetting about that,' I

say. 'I don't know what's wrong with me at the moment. I don't feel like classic Emily. It feels like all these little things keep piling up to make me question myself, to make me feel insecure when I don't want to. Whether it's my mum's stuff worming its way into my brain, or massively overthinking everything about Joe, or even some random dude on the street calling me a fat bitch, which was *ages* ago, but it's just all working together to stress me out. I feel like I should be better than all of this, that in my heart I know I *am* better than all of this, but also it's really hard sometimes to feel like I'm keeping my head above water.'

'That's a lot you've got going on, pal.' Camila sighs, hoisting herself up on the bed next to me. She reaches out to stroke my arm.

'Yeah.'

'Let's start with one item on the list. So, you're stressed and need someone to calm you down about making a move on Joe, right?'

'Right. But it sort of doesn't seem that important now. I feel like an actual idiot for kissing him, and I really wish I had just left it alone and not tried to push my luck . . . To be honest, I'm just happy to see you.'

'Wait, catch me up. What's gone on with him since we last spoke? It sounds like you two have got pretty close if you're going around trying to kiss him.'

I go over to my record player and put on the Hairpins record Joe gave me, sit back down next to Camila, take a deep breath, and begin to fill her in. And she listens. And she makes me feel better. She calms me, makes me feel like it's, well, in the words of the Hairpins, like it's 'No Big Deal'.

We spend the rest of the evening just chatting. About boys, about school, about what'll happen next year, about music. She might not be as high energy as Abi, but she's comforting to have around, and I'm grateful to have her back in my life.

Alone in my room later that night after Camila has left, I lie back on my bed and put the record back to the beginning. I let myself slip gloriously into the relentless, jagged fuzz of the music and Lee Klein's wild voice and try to empty my mind of thoughts. There's too much going on in there. But at least now Camila is one less thing to worry about.

# CHAPTER SIXTEEN

'That's Us/Wild Combination' –
Arthur Russell

The next day, I stop by Beats Per Minute uninvited. I say 'stop by'. That makes it sound like I was just passing, rather than deliberately going into Croydon at the end of Joe's working day to make sure I got to the shop when there would be no customers to distract him. I wanted this to be as precise and rehearsed as my kiss was uncontrolled and spontaneous.

The words go around in my head: *I'msorryitwasamistake-Ididn'twanttomakeyoufeeluncomfortable*. A carousel of apologies and backtracking. I know it's not brave of me, but I just want us to be able to pretend it didn't happen, to just go back to normal. Shove the awkwardness back into its box.

I'm wearing a red tea dress with leopard-print flats in the hope that it instils some kind of power and confidence in me. Fake it till you make it.

I reach Beats Per Minute exactly as planned, ten minutes before it closes, and I'm relieved to find it's not shut already. Breathe, Emily. Just say what you came here to say. Take control of this situation. Don't sit at home wondering what he's thinking. Just stay calm and be the boss.

Pushing open the door, I can see that the shop is empty of customers, but, thank God, not empty of Joe. My heart skips a beat. He jumps up from the stool behind the counter and brushes off his jumper, like he doesn't know what to do with his hands.

'Can I . . . help you?' he asks awkwardly.

I clear my throat and take a breath. 'I'm sorry about yesterday. I didn't mean to make you feel uncomfortable,' I say calmly. Might as well just launch into it so I don't chicken out. 'I've really enjoyed getting to know you, and I'm sorry if, in one moment of madness, I made you feel like you don't want to hang out with me any more. I had started to see you as a friend. Someone I enjoy spending time with. And I don't want to have to just throw that away because of . . . well, the thing. But I understand if you think it's weird and don't want to hang out any more.' I roll a loose thread from the hem of my dress between my fingers.

Joe just stares at me. The wait for him to speak feels interminable.

'Oh . . .' he says.

*Oh*. Is that *it*?

'Oh, what?' I reply slightly too quickly out of irritation. Keep it cool, Emily. Don't let your nerves get the better of you.

'I . . . guess I had a slightly different view on it,' he says, 'but if that's how you feel, then . . .'

'Try me,' I say decisively.

'I actually wanted to apologize to you myself,' he says. 'For reacting the way I did. Or rather, for not reacting.'

I made such an effort to be clear with him, and now he repays me with this cryptic chat? I try to unpick it in my brain as he walks over to the door and flips the 'Open' sign to 'Closed' before continuing, leaning his back against the plate glass, keeping a distance between us.

'It was especially weird of me because you did the exact thing I had wanted to do all evening but hadn't found the right moment for. I think I've . . . like . . . I don't know . . . I guess you could say I've developed feelings for you.'

My mouth goes dry. I feel nauseous. I have a funny feeling I'm the one making the blank, surprised face right now.

'But I get it if you just want to be friends,' he says. 'I had been wondering what would be the right thing to do.'

What's the most cool, chilled-out way that I can leap into his arms and smother his face in kisses and say, *No no no — all I want is for you to love me forever. Kiss me now and never stop?*

'Whatever you think is best,' I say. What? No! That's not being the boss! That's too chilled out. I don't want him to think I don't care. My ongoing problem is I care a bit too much.

Joe stands up straighter. He looks me in the eye and opens his mouth to speak.

'No, wait . . .' I begin again.

I'm not going to let this opportunity slip out of my hands because I'm scared. What am I scared of anyway? Scared of putting myself out there; scared of doing something other than 'play it cool'; scared of comparing myself to the other girls in his life; scared to believe that someone could be interested in me even though I'm fat. Those are not things I want to be scared of even though they might be true, and I'm not going to let them get the better of me this time.

'Feelings,' I say, swallowing, trying to buy time. 'I have feelings for you, too. I feel a lot for you. And I don't just want to be your friend. Not that that's not good enough . . . God, I hate that expression. It makes it sound like "friends" is such a chore, just a consolation prize for, I don't know, romance and stuff. But I want to be your friend, and I want to try all that other stuff too, with you.' Wow, I really went for it. I want to close my eyes so I don't have to see Joe's reaction. Did I go too far?

Joe opens his arms. 'Come here,' he says.

And I walk to him. It feels like the longest three steps of my life. I stand in front of him, wondering what comes next and wondering why I feel like it's up to him. He pulls me in and kisses me. Properly kisses me. Not the second-long, closed-mouth, chaste peck of last night. This is something else. Something new. Something soft and warm. Something that manages to be comforting and exciting all at the same time. My heart races; my head spins. I'm glad his arms are around me so that I don't just collapse to the floor in shock.

We finally pull apart, and I can't help but laugh.

'What are you laughing at?' Joe asks, awkwardly stroking my hair.

I can only assume it'll get less awkward when we get used to each other.

'I don't know. I guess because I thought I was coming here to clear the air and clear my name of being a little weirdo pouncing on you last night,' I say.

'And instead you got pounced on,' he replies, smiling.

'Yeah. I like to think I know everything, but it feels like lately I don't know anything.' I shake my head. 'This has been a good kind of surprise.'

'Yes,' he says, and wraps his arms around me again.

We kiss for what feels like an eternity. He links his fingers through mine. I've never held hands with anyone before.

Joe pulls back to look at me. 'You know, the first time you came here, I was trying so hard to play it cool that I even pretended I couldn't remember your name.'

'So, you thought I was cute even then?' I'm stunned.

'Yeah . . . I guess so . . .' Joe blushes and looks down at his shoes.

'So . . .' I venture, preparing to bring up a world that is outside this room. 'What shall we do now? Are you busy tonight?'

'Some mates are going for a drink. I said I'd meet them about now,' he says with a grimace, looking down at his watch.

Shot down instantly. I hope my disappointment doesn't show on my face.

'They're back from uni because it's reading week. I shouldn't really miss it.'

'Oh, that's OK.' I wave it off. It's not important.

'I'm sorry . . . Obviously I would have loved to hang out with you,' he says, swooping an arm around my waist and pressing his mouth on mine again.

I melt. Again.

'So, when do you want to hang out?' I say. I'm determined not to end today without knowing when I'll see Joe again, especially now it's going to be extra fun to be around him.

'I can do Monday night, after work? If you want to come to mine?' he asks, raising his eyebrows expectantly.

What does that mean? Does that mean, like . . . to his house? To his room? To his bed? So this is how he got so many girls into bed before. Just by asking them. But we only just kissed, so maybe he didn't mean that at all.

'Ummm, Monday's fine, but . . . maybe we could just meet for a drink or dinner or something?' I say, desperately hoping that saying no to one part doesn't mean jeopardizing the whole thing.

Joe's face falls for a second, but he recovers quickly.

'Yeah, yeah, of course,' he says. 'We can meet wherever you want.'

'OK, I'll message you,' I say. 'I guess I should leave you to go and meet your mates now.'

He pulls me in again and kisses me and kisses me, and it feels just as amazing, even when it's not a surprise.

'I don't want to have to leave you,' he says. 'This is just bad timing. I can't wait to see you on Monday.'

'It's OK – I get it,' I say. One more kiss. Now we've started, I just don't ever want to stop. 'Which pub are you meeting your friends at?'

'The Fox,' Joe says distractedly, fishing around in his backpack for the keys to lock up the shop. 'Why?'

'Oh, that's opposite my bus stop. I'll walk with you.'

'You don't have to do that,' Joe says.

Beats Per Minute is all locked up, and we're ready to hit the road.

'It's literally opposite, and I'm walking there anyway,' I say.

And he knows this already; he left me there only last night after The Kiss.

'Sure, of course.' He sounds flustered, but nothing can dampen my mood now.

It's only a couple of minutes' walk away, but I feel like I'm fizzing with happiness to be walking the streets of beautiful Croydon with a cute guy I'm crazy about who, in his own words, has *feelings* for me. I look down at his hand dangling by his side as he walks next to me, but before I can reach out for it, he stuffs it into his jacket pocket. I guess it's cold out.

We're at our destination in no time: my bus stop on one side of the road; his pub on the other.

'Well, bye then,' I say, smiling coyly at him. Well, as coyly as I can manage.

'I'll see you Monday,' he says firmly, looking me in the eye.

I reach up to kiss him, and he kisses me back, but I sense a resistance this time. It's probably nothing. I refuse to worry about *nothing*. I turn to cross the road, and in the reflection of a passing bus, see Joe glancing over his shoulder before he walks up the stone steps to the pub.

Having spent most of Sunday in a daze, Monday comes around like a rude slap in the face. I'm spending most of the day in a state of heightened distraction, daydreaming my way through my classes. Even getting ninety-five per cent on a physics test doesn't come close to how happy I feel every time I think of Joe. Not that I can forget Joe even for a second. The happy little buzz is always there in the back of my mind. I'm not even scared he's going to cancel on me any more. I'm all optimism. Pure good vibes.

And he doesn't cancel. He messages me at lunchtime telling me to meet him at the Fox for a drink, and when I arrive, he's already sitting at one of the tables near the back, reading.

My first proper, actual, confirmed date with Joe.

My heart is thumping in my chest as I make my way across the pub. He looks up, and our eyes meet, and it's just the most limitless kind of excitement. Chemical. He shoves his copy of *A Clockwork Orange* into his backpack and runs his hands through his messy blond hair as he gets up to greet me.

I want him to take me in his arms and kiss me on the mouth so I can melt into him again. But instead we hug awkwardly, and he brushes his lips against my cheek. Oh well, the night is young. We'll warm up.

And we do warm up. Conversation flows easily between us: no awkward silences. Just an endless back and forth of effortless chat and swooning glances and electrical charge. I knew I wasn't wrong about him. From the first moment I saw him at Ben's party only a few months ago, I knew I had to find a way to get him in my life and keep him here.

All the talking has been keeping us occupied, and before we know it an hour flies by, and we suddenly realize we've finished our drinks. Joe's about to head up to the bar to order another round when he leaps out of his seat. I look around for the cause of the excitement and see a tall black guy in a rugby shirt approaching our table with a smile on his face. Joe dashes forward and intercepts him with an enthusiastic greeting.

'Matt!'

'Come here often?' Matt says, slapping Joe on the back and drawing him into a hug. 'I only left you here, what, twenty hours ago?'

'Can't keep me away, buddy. What are you up to?'

It doesn't take a sleuth to figure out this is one of the friends he met yesterday.

'Just meeting Danny here for a drink, seeing as he couldn't make it on Saturday night. Thought I'd catch him for a little one-on-one time tonight.'

'Oh cool – you'll have a good time. He seems really happy at the moment,' Joe says.

I crane my neck, wondering when Joe's going to introduce me.

'Yeah, man! I've missed him,' Matt says. 'And I've even

missed his non-stop table-top drumming.' He breaks Joe's gaze and flicks a warm glance in my direction, his eyebrows raised. 'So, who's—?'

'We were just leaving, actually,' Joe says, nearly tripping over his own feet in the hurry to grab his coat and backpack.

I lock eyes with Matt and shrug mutely as Joe grabs my arm, and I find myself being bundled towards the exit.

'See you soon though?' Joe calls over his shoulder.

Once outside, Joe turns to me. 'I thought we could move somewhere else for another one,' he says, as if nothing weird has just happened.

'Um . . . sure . . .' I can't manage much better than that.

Joe leads me round the corner to the White Horse, where, mercifully, there is no bouncer checking IDs tonight.

'Who was that guy?' I ask.

'Oh, just my friend Matt.'

That's it. That's all the explanation I'm going to get out of him – I can tell.

I swallow down any more questions, and we go inside the pub, sliding into the first empty booth. But the atmosphere has changed in an instant. The air is prickling between us, heavy with all my expectations, all my desires for him to love me, to touch me, to want me. I'm starting to question if that conversation on Saturday night even happened. But I know it did. Maybe I'm just being weird and prickly and difficult and demanding. What right do I have to be demanding anyway? I got what I wanted! Joe is 'into me'. Joe even kisses me, which feels like the greatest prize of all.

I decide not to push him and make it even more awkward and instead head to the bar to get us some drinks.

'So . . . do you want to come to mine next weekend?' Joe asks casually as we're heading out of the pub after a slightly tense drink.

My heart leaps back into action, hammering against my ribcage. Does this mean I'll have to wait nearly a whole week to see him? Or, wait . . . Does it mean . . . ? Oh man. It means he still wants to be alone with me, in his bedroom. And soon . . . I don't hesitate too long in case he retracts the offer.

'Yes. I do. Next weekend is fine,' I say quickly as we cross over the road to my bus stop.

'Great. I'll message you my address. It'll be fun,' he says, grinning at me.

And with that, he gives me a quick hug, turns on his heel, and makes his way down the road. I watch him go, confused. After virtually nothing for months, I'm struggling to get my head around his newfound keenness.

As I wait for the bus, my phone screen illuminates in my hand. But it's not Joe messaging me his address; it's a call from Katie. I watch as it rings silently in front of me, but I don't pick up, and I'm not sure why. I wait until I'm on the bus and then I fire off an email to her, apologizing for not picking up. But I can't help myself: I add a few sentences about my current fears and anxieties, just enough to say how I'm feeling, maybe enough to provoke a little sisterly advice. Just a little word-vomit to get it all out of my system, and then I can go back to normal. I should try not to think about my weird worries. My fears.

He's keen now. That's all that matters.

# CHAPTER SEVENTEEN

'Let's Talk About Sex' – Salt-N-Pepa

I'd always imagined that the day after being propositioned by a crush, I'd wake up feeling like I was floating on a fluffy cloud of happiness . . . But nope. Instead, I wake with a start, a tightness gripping at my chest. Sex. I need to get my life together. Because I might, maybe, have sex with Joe soon . . . right? Even though his behaviour last night seemed kind of *weird*, that's where this is headed, I'm almost sure of it. I should be excited, shouldn't I? But I guess it's normal to feel nervous as well. Normal. That's the aim of the game. I just want to feel *normal*. How do I figure all this out? I'm pretty sure that if I google *'How do I have sex?'* it's just going to turn up a load of porn. So that's out. I need some actual human input, and I know just the person to ask: Abi.

> I need help.

A reply comes quickly.

Abi

 I am here. Tell me what you need.

We arrange a lunchtime trip to McDonald's so I can grill her in private without my parents or hostile Holly-shaped ears listening in. I'm starting to feel better about everything already.

I'm sitting in our form room waiting for morning registration, when Abi slides into the seat next to me and whispers, 'What's up?' in my ear. I tell her we can talk later. I don't want to waste any of her golden thoughts when I'm not a hundred per cent focused. This is too important.

But first, English class. I've loitered too long in the form room and, by the time I arrive, the only seat left is next to Holly. Kill me. She completely unnecessarily moves her chair extra inches to the side, just in case there was any way I could forget that I'm a gross fat person who takes up extra space.

Low-key goth Mrs Mackinnon arrives clutching a stack of dog-eared printouts. Oh no, we're getting our essays back today. My almost-forgotten essay. My night-before essay. Double kill me.

'These very much varied in quality,' she begins.

Uh oh.

'But in general, they bode well for the essays you'll write towards the end of term. I think it'll do you good if we go over a few themes in particular, but we can cover those in more detail nearer the time that you have to write your coursework.'

All I'm hearing is that there's time to salvage the outcome of my actual coursework. All is not lost. Mrs Mackinnon swishes around the room in her gauzy black skirt, distributing marked essays to their authors. She places mine face up on my desk, and I brace myself.

Her red writing leaps out at me: *This was a joy to read. Spirited, original, fizzing with a real energy. A few typos – please be more careful and PROOFREAD next time!*

. . . Wait. There's an 'A' in a circle.

I check and double check that she hasn't given me someone else's essay. She hasn't. I can feel the stress leaving my body: I got away with it. Even basking in the glory of my own surprise victory, I can't help but steal a glance at Holly's paper. I manage to catch it just before she turns it over with an audible huff: *Needs MUCH closer reading of the texts, but a good attempt. Watch your sentence formation. Not such a good handle on Sassoon – C+.*

I feel bad because I feel . . . good. I bashed this out in four hours in the middle of the night. If I can produce something that's 'a joy to read' with minimal effort, then I can probably go one better if I put a bit of time and concentration in.

I quickly wipe the smile off my face when I catch Holly looking at me. I don't want to rub it in, after all.

When the bell rings at the end of class, Mrs Mackinnon tells me to stay back. I brace myself for a lecture, although on what, I'm not sure yet. I wonder if the 'I'm-in-trouble' reflex is something you ever grow out of.

'Emily, you did so well in your AS levels,' she begins. 'Across the board. We were all really impressed with you. Sometimes you give the impression you're not really listening, but you can clearly make up for that in your own time.'

'Oh. Thanks, Mrs Mackinnon,' I reply, profoundly surprised. I mean, I know I did well in my AS levels, but I didn't know they had been the topic of staffroom conversation.

'I don't know if this is something you're thinking about, but I just wanted to make sure you're not planning on selling yourself short next year.' She gathers up her textbooks and clutches them close to her chest, her long dyed-black hair trailing in a ponytail over her shoulder.

'What do you mean, selling myself short?'

'I mean don't be too influenced by what your friends are doing. Don't settle. Make sure you're following your own path, whatever that is. Your next step after school is a big decision, and you have every option open to you. I know Mrs Shah is as keen for you to pursue physics as I am for you to keep studying English. Your talents are wide-ranging and diverse.'

She looks so serious now that I almost want to laugh the nervous laugh of someone not used to taking things seriously. For all my blasé attitude, it's weird to be in the direct beam of someone's attention. But more than that, I feel warmed that she's so serious in her belief in me.

'Yes, I understand. I'm sure I'll make the right choice,' I say.

And I realize that I actually mean it. That over the past few days, everything has sort of settled, and I know who I am and what I want and, I hope, what my future looks like.

'Your essay was great. I've been really taken with your work in the past,' she says, 'but this was so lively. I'd love to see more of that this year.'

'I appreciate your support,' I say stiffly, looking at my shoes.

I'm relieved to be feeling good about something that isn't Joe. There is more to my life than him. But I can't pretend he isn't occupying a fair bit of brain space right now. With a grateful smile, I pick up my bag and my essay and head out of the classroom. Things are looking up already, and I don't want to let a boy ruin things.

Before I know it, it's lunchtime, and thoughts of Joe can legitimately invade my brain. It's time for my McDonald's conference with Abi.

'Nuggs are on me, pal,' I say, tapping my contactless card with a flourish.

The least I can do in exchange for asking Abi lots of extremely personal questions is cough up for her lunch. We settle at a table near the window as we both have a natural thirst to know what's going on around us. Some could call it nosiness.

'So. Here's the deal,' I begin, unwrapping my double cheeseburger. 'Things are going well with Joe. Finally. He has confessed that he fancies me – tick,' I say, tracing a tick in the air. 'We have made out, on more than one occasion – tick. And now I am . . . keen to . . . seal the deal, so to speak.'

I'm trying to stop thinking about what happened with Matt in the pub. I don't want to muddy the water by bringing up my little nagging fear that Joe might be ashamed of me. I'm trying to be satisfied that I have him. Abi doesn't need to know about my insecurities.

'That's so great,' she says, seemingly overcome with happiness for her useless friend Emily. 'I knew this wasn't a lost cause! No matter how many times you said it was, I *knew* that he had to feel something for you. Anyway . . . how can I be of assistance?'

'I guess I just want to find out . . . what to expect when we eventually . . . Like, sex-wise, you know? I . . . don't

234

know what's expected of me,' I say. 'Sorry – I feel really stupid even asking, like I should know all this stuff already. But I don't.'

As Abi listens to my words, her expression changes. She looks like a deer in headlights, which is not the gleefully salacious response I was expecting.

'Well . . . Maybe I'm not the best person to ask . . .' she says after a long pause.

'What's that supposed to mean? You are –' I raise my eyebrows – 'extremely qualified.'

Abi starts playing with her food, lining her chips up around the edge of the nugget box. 'Actually, no. I'm not,' she says. She looks up from her chicken nuggets and meets my eyes. 'I haven't . . . actually . . .'

Is she joking? What's this about?

'So, you're saying you've never . . . Like, never . . .' I trail off, suddenly self-conscious about probing her on this now that it seems like it's something of a sore spot.

'Don't make me say it out loud.' She drops her voice to a whisper, in case the patrons of Church Street McDonald's have nothing better to do than eavesdrop on two girls eating lunch.

'OK, OK – I won't . . . But are you really saying you haven't had sex with . . . anyone? Not Oliver? None of the guys before him?'

'No, no – things never lasted long enough with anyone

235

else,' she says, shaking her head. 'I want it to be special, and it's never felt special.'

'That makes sense,' I say, nodding fervently. It does make sense. I mean, I'm not expecting candlelight and rose petals with Joe, but I've never second-guessed whether I want to sleep with him. And that feels special enough. 'But you . . . always let me assume you had. Even if you didn't explicitly say, "I have had sex." It was just a thing that seemed to go without saying, you know?' I shift in my seat.

She stirs her milkshake. 'Yeah . . . I know,' she says. 'I'm sorry I lied.'

'No, mate! You didn't lie . . .' I reach across the table and stroke her hand. I don't want her to feel guilty about this of all things. I was just hoping she'd be able to give me some solid advice on the art of seduction. 'I guess I got it into my head that everyone was having sex all the time except me.'

'Yes! That's it, isn't it? That's the whole problem . . .' Abi says. 'I think Oliver thinks we should have done it by now, even though we're not, like, *official*. But I just don't want to. I don't feel right about it.' Her voice is shaking now.

God – poor Abi. I feel so bad for her.

'Don't do anything you don't want to do. Jesus. You've held out this long, a little longer won't hurt anyone,' I say, as if I'm an expert on the matter. 'Your happiness and your comfort are the most important things here. If Oliver can't deal with that, then he isn't worthy of you. You're a princess. You're a queen.'

Abi sighs. 'I just don't want to let him down. I don't want to lose him. I like him . . . but I'm nervous.'

'You wouldn't be letting anyone down. This is too important for you to rush into when you're saying that you're nervous, not ready, scared. Comfort should be the bare minimum, you know? At least feel comfortable . . .' I trail off.

'God, what a disappointment I must be,' she says, wiping her eyes on the sleeve of her jumper and smiling. 'You came to me asking for advice about sex, and instead you've ended up having to give me advice.'

I don't feel disappointed at all. It's a relief to know that I'm not the last person in the world to have sex. But I must admit, this did not go the way I thought it would. And I'm still none the wiser. Instead of returning to the afternoon's lessons victorious in my wisdom, I feel kind of unnerved as we collect up our stuff and begin our walk back round the corner to school.

'Do we have to go back?' I moan. 'I don't want to have to tell Mrs Mackinnon that I haven't sent off my UCAS form yet.'

'Oh, is it university chat again this afternoon? At least that means I can sneak off.'

'Ugh! I should have applied to Oxford or Cambridge purely because it would have forced me to get my butt in gear months ago.'

'Yes, except you would literally hate being anywhere other than London, so that's a good reason to not jump through all those hoops.'

'You know me too well. Do you think I'm being stupid, though?' I nibble the skin on my lip. 'Not wanting some big adventure in, like, Edinburgh or Belfast or whatever?'

'What's fun about an adventure you don't want to go on?' Abi says, shrugging.

We're approaching the gates to the sixth-form block when we see someone sitting hunched up on the wall outside. A sound of sniffling becomes more audible the closer we get. Simultaneously Abi and I realize it's Holly, and we both groan quietly. This had better not be about her mock English essay.

'Should we stop? Do we have to be nice to her?' I whisper to Abi as we slow our pace to buy time.

'I really, really don't want to, but I also want to get into heaven,' she whispers back.

'Fine, fine.' We can't delay it any longer. We have to bite the bullet.

We stop in front of Holly and try not to loom too ominously over her.

'Hi, Holly,' Abi says softly.

'H-h-hi,' she chokes between sniffles. 'Not going to beat me up again, are you, Emily?' she says with a smile, clearly still incapable of hiding her true self even while openly weeping.

'Um, no, I wasn't planning to,' I say, glancing shiftily at Abi, the only witness to my bathroom run-in with Holly. 'You want to talk about it?'

'Not to you two,' she says bitterly.

All right then. Abi will still get into heaven, and we don't have to hear about Horrible Holly's problems: a win-win.

'We're not as bad as we seem, I promise,' says Abi.

We're not bad at all! Why is she feeding Holly's fiction?

'Ugh, fine,' Holly says, rolling her eyes and throwing her snotty tissue on the ground next to her. 'It sounds so stupid, but I got rejected from the uni I wanted to go to today. Already. They must have had my application for a week, max.'

'Oh no, I'm sorry,' I say. God. I thought her mum must have been murdered or, at the very least, someone had stolen her cat. This is containable misery. She'll get over it. I don't have to spend too much time feeling sorry for her.

'I just don't know what more I have to do,' she says, shaking her head, running her fingers through her sleek, glossy light brown hair. 'I so wanted to go to uni in London, and now it's just off the table.'

Right, that's decided: I'll only apply to London

universities so that I can at least be safe in the knowledge I won't have to be anywhere near Holly ever again.

'It's a gamble, man,' says Abi, taking a seat on the wall next to her, leaving me loitering awkwardly.

I'm hoping we won't be here long enough to warrant my having to sit down too.

'Anyway, even if you have the grades, it doesn't guarantee anything. Who knows what they're looking for any more.'

Holly sighs. 'You're right. I think I'd just got my hopes up because . . . well, I *am* one of the cleverest in the year. But that doesn't guarantee anything, I suppose,' she says.

Holly stands up, and together we begin the long stomp up the stairs to the sixth-form block. When we get to the top of the stairs, she heads off towards the bathroom, stopping abruptly just outside its door. She turns around, fixing us with a serious stare.

'Don't you dare tell anyone I was crying,' she says, her eyes flashing.

She really seems to mean it. So many tears today, there must be something in the water.

'Your secret's safe with us, Holly,' I say, as kindly as I can. It might be a nice little break for me if she could turn her attentions to someone else for a while. Fingers crossed this has earned me at least a couple of weeks without one of her little jibes.

'Thanks . . .' she says, barging the bathroom door open.

'God, I really hope I never care that much about uni,' I say as we head to the common room.

That afternoon, for the crime of not having sent off my UCAS form yet, I'm treated to university chat and more university chat. Abi gets to slink off to our form room and time-waste her way through the afternoon, but Ella, Sophia, Camila and I have to confront our futures.

The longer I sit there listening to all the personal-statement advice, all the convoluted point conversions, all the tactical guidance, the more I'm sure that finally I know what I'm doing. English it is. UCL it is.

# CHAPTER EIGHTEEN

'Because the Night' – Patti Smith

Abi's lack of practical advice the other day was something of a setback, but there's nothing I can do about that now. The day is here: I am going to Joe's house. Possibly to have sex with him – that's still an unknown. I'm beyond grateful that my parents are out when I leave, so I don't have to answer any awkward questions about where I'm going. I'm such a bad liar, and as much as I like my mum and dad, I really don't fancy talking about it with them.

Just before I leave the house, I check my phone for a last-minute cancellation from Joe (I just can't shake that fear) and instead find a text from my aunt.

Aunt Isobel

> Great news, beautiful niece!
> Told Dickhead Dennis it was over.

Huh. This puts a spring in my step as I stomp to the bus stop. Once I'm on the right bus (don't want to get distracted and end up in Crawley), I disappear into my thoughts – Am I too fat to have sex? Has he ever seen a fat body before? What if I crush him? – and before I know it, I have to get off.

Oh God. I'm already at Joe's. I look at my watch: bang on time. There's nowhere to go from here but onwards. It's time. Yes, my time has come. There's a good chance I am going to have sex with a human male today. And a human male I really fancy, no less. Am I nervous? Yes. So nervous I could throw up. But I'm absolutely not going to back out now . . .

I slowly climb the little set of stone steps to his front door. I press the doorbell and almost jerk back in fright when my mechanical, robot-like motion triggers an insistent high-pitched buzz on the other side of the door. My nerves are jangling, I'm so unbelievably on edge.

And suddenly there he is. Right in front of me, in a white T-shirt and black jeans and odd socks. A halo of dirty blond hair around his head, his ugly-sexy glasses on. Too much for me to take. I am absolutely going to have sex with this boy today. Even though he invited me over, he seems genuinely surprised to see me standing there on his doorstep, like I'm a special present that's turned up without warning. Before we can even greet each other, he's got his arms around me and is kissing me like our days on earth are numbered. I don't want to take my hands off him – I just want to stay like this forever and ever. Because if we just stay like this, just keep kissing and don't break apart, then maybe I won't have to take my clothes off in front of him.

I'm torn. I want to have done it, but I don't want to actually do it. I want it to be a thing I've done but . . . Do I want to live through the actual experience of doing it? As I stand there kissing him on the welcome mat, I'm still not sure.

'No one's home,' he says, grinning at me as he leads me into the kitchen.

'Oh, that's cool,' I say. I feel a lump in my throat. A kind of rising panic. All alone. Definitely on purpose. This is definitely a sex visit.

As I watch Joe pour me a drink, scenes flash across my mind like soft porn being beamed on to a huge cinema screen. Girls girls girls: slim, tall, sexy, cool girls, writhing seductively, giggling coquettishly, stripping off, climbing on top of him. I feel faint and overwhelmed. I am not one of them. I do not deserve to be here. But I'm not going to tell him that. What's important is that I just get through it. I gulp my drink down too fast. I should have sipped it, prolonged the preamble. But now it's gone, and now we're going upstairs, and now I'm going to have to take my clothes off, and now he's going to find out I have no idea what I'm doing. No idea at all.

I'm surprised by how tidy his bedroom is. Clearly

that is not something we have in common. But the walls are covered with the same range of sun-faded posters as Beats Per Minute: peeling old artwork advertising albums from years ago. Am I going to lose my virginity under the gaze of David Byrne from decades-old Talking Heads promotional material? Possibly. The silence is kind of painful. Why hasn't he put some music on? He, of all people. Now, of all the moments. Just something to fill the void where our nervousness has created a yawning chasm of awkwardness.

But no. The silence stretches between us.

I had sort of assumed we would sit and chat awkwardly for a bit before getting down to it, but no. There's no time for awkward chat. Joe wants to get on with it. So, I wasn't imagining it before, right? He *is* into me. He literally wants to have sex with me. He's interested in me. He wants me! I feel giddy with disbelief, totally overcome with the knowledge that I am right here right now with Joe. In his bedroom. Making out with him.

He pulls his shirt off over his head, locking eyes with me and smiling. I take in the slim softness of his body, my pleasure tinged with the fear of knowing it'll be my turn in no time at all. We kiss, his hand cupped around the back of my head, drawing me towards him. I feel like we could fuse together.

It's time. It's my turn. We have been moving towards this point since I walked through the door, and now we are finally here, and I can't escape. Joe is fumbling with the buttons on my shirt, running his hands over my body. I wonder if he can feel my heart beating through my chest. Let's be real, though: that's probably not what he's really interested in right now. My shirt is off, fluttering to the floor, and we're still kissing, his hands still on me, wrapped around my waist. This is not Ryan, part two. Joe is really touching me; he's really here.

He takes me by the hand and guides me to his bed. It's only a single bed, and we giggle awkwardly as we try to lie down on it. I'm blushing furiously, even more acutely aware that I take up a lot of room. I try to put the thought out of my mind. I want to be present, to feel everything about this moment. But the focus of my mind keeps flicking around, the good, the bad, the scary, the exciting. I can't stay present. I want to be here, but I can't keep myself here – there's just too much of everything in my mind.

Here we are on this tiny mattress: me in my bra and jeans; him in his jeans and socks . . . on top of me, kissing me. I wish I could be on top of him, but I can't get over the fear that I would crush him. Of course you wouldn't crush him, you idiot. But then again, you might. What do you know about this, Emily?

He pulls at the waistband of my jeans, so I take the hint and wriggle out of them. More awkward laughter to cover the real awkwardness. But it doesn't kill the mood for too long, and I feel him brush over the outside of my black Marks and Spencer granny pants, and a tingle of pleasure washes over me. I want this. I want more of this. But – oh my God – why didn't I wear something sexier? No time to think about that now. Just switch off and feel everything with him. But like a bad dream that floats back to you the next day, there on the projector screen in my brain is him and 'the girls'. The girls. The girls. Slim and sexy and sleek-haired with noses pierced, carelessly dressed and so cool. Nothing like me. How can he not be judging me right now?

'Are you OK?' he asks, drawing back.

'Um . . . yeah. I'm fine.' I don't want to kill the moment. Shut up, stupid insecurities. Don't ruin this. You want this. 'Why? Aren't you?'

'You don't seem fine right now,' he says, his voice tinged with frustration, urgency.

I sigh. I don't know what to say.

'You seem like you're not really *here*.'

'I'm just thinking about . . .' I pause. I can't say it out loud. It's just too pathetic. Too desperately sad. I draw myself up into a sitting position. I am officially causing this to grind to a halt.

'What?' Joe asks me, his eyes big and imploring.

'The girls, I guess.' I stare down at my bare feet dangling over the carpet. The chipped red nail varnish. The chubby ankles. The bits that I missed shaving. 'I'm just scared I can't live up to the girls you've been with.'

'What are you talking about? Who are you talking about?' he asks impatiently.

I move to the edge of the bed, shivering in my underwear, acutely aware of the doughy excess of my skin, all covered in goosebumps.

'You know, the girls. All the girls . . . before,' I say. I don't want to look him in the eye. I'm so embarrassed of my body – my big, lumpy, pale body. I feel ashamed as I imagine it in comparison to what he must be used to. In comparison to what he *expects* a girl's body to look like.

But Joe is still looking at me with a confused expression. And then a change comes over his face as though the cogs in his mind have suddenly clicked into place.

'Oh my God . . . has Oliver said something to you? Is that what this is about? That was . . . never true,' he says, shaking his head and pressing the heels of his palms into his eyes out of apparent frustration.

'What do you mean?' My heart is pounding a thousand beats a minute.

'Argh, Emily . . . that was just a dumb deliberate rumour –

a stupid lie Oliver came up with because he thought it would make it easier for me to get with girls. He said it didn't matter if I actually hadn't as long as people thought I had. And then I guess people believed it, and I just never bothered to correct them . . .' He looks up at me with his stupid, horrible blue eyes.

'But . . . *I* believed it . . .' I kind of feel sick. And I feel like an idiot. But why should I? It's *him* that should be embarrassed about spreading such a stupid lie.

He pushes his hair back from his face. 'I thought it would make girls want to sleep with me more, but now it's making you want to sleep with me less,' he says, articulating exactly what I'm thinking.

I hadn't wanted to sleep with him because I thought he was too experienced. And now I know that's not true, where does that leave me?

'I . . . I do. I do want to sleep with you. I'm glad we're here,' I say. 'I like you so much.'

First Abi – now him. Has anyone in the world actually had sex? Or is it all a huge lie that was invented to make me feel like the odd one out? I thought this was meant to be a cool, easy exchange of bodily fluids. Why does it have to be so complicated?

'I like you too,' he says, sitting up and tentatively putting an arm around me.

In that moment, I feel safe and important. He's stupid, and he made a bad decision. That's not so bad, is it?

I smile at him. 'Good. So, we can keep . . . hanging out?'

'Totally. I think you're amazing,' he says.

I can't stop myself from smiling, even if nothing about this evening went the way I thought it would.

He pulls me towards him and kisses me with an intensity I haven't felt before, stopping briefly to look me in the eyes. 'Shall we chill today and come back to this another time?'

'Yes. There will be other times,' I say assertively, as much to reassure myself as to reassure him.


Even though I had wanted to sleep with him tonight, I can't pretend that I don't feel a weird sense of relief as I put my clothes back on. Maybe he was expecting me to just hang out in my underwear, but it would feel too weird. I would be too self-conscious. We sit on the bed and watch a DVD of *Brass Eye*. I've seen it before, and I'm not really concentrating. Now that we are clearly not going to have sex today, I feel like I've cheated myself out of a Major Life Experience. This was my chance to enter the world of the sex-havers! Actual sex with actual Joe! But it's been a bumpy road to get here. Maybe it's not such a bad idea to wait.

# CHAPTER NINETEEN

'Dancing on My Own' – Robyn

Everything is coming up Emily. Christmas is so nearly here, for the past few weeks I've have a maybe-boyfriend who I make out with and listen to records with at Beats Per Minute every Thursday night after it closes (no sex yet, but I think it's heading that way soon), and I've made it to the end of term in one piece. School's out and it's officially the Christmas holidays, and I could not be happier about it. I don't even care about mock exams after the break. All I care about is Oliver's party tonight and the fact that Joe is going, and we will be out in the world together. That makes it real, right?

OK, outfit time. Hmm. What to wear? A slouchy, oversized shirt and tight jeans, I reckon. I think about Joe as I dress, wondering if he prefers it when I wear something more feminine or prettier or whatever. I look at myself in the mirror and like what I see, hoping he will too. I go downstairs and pick up my bag, but just as I'm about to head out the door, I turn on my heel, run back upstairs and switch the jeans for a stretchy jersey skirt. It doesn't conceal the fat around my hips, but it is more girly. I'll take it.

I arrive at the party at the same time as Ella and Sophia, who profess their excitement at finally being properly introduced to 'my man'. I blush and tell them to shut up, but in reality, I can't help but feel the warm glow of something like pride at the thought. *My man*. It feels good to be someone who other people are excited for. I'm not used to this.

When we make it inside, Abi is already there, and the party seems to be in full swing. Camila and Ryan look cosy on a sofa, but both quickly leap up to hug me. Even Ryan has shaken off his awkwardness around me. My heart leaps as I wonder if Joe is here already. My man.

Even though we all saw each other at school a matter of hours ago, we seem to have loads to talk about, and we gossip so excitedly, I temporarily forget about Joe. We knock back our blue alcopops in record time (embracing the spirit of Christmas), and I volunteer to get us a refill. I squeeze past a group of people loitering in the kitchen doorway to get to the fridge where our fluorescent blue bottles are chilling like a fine wine. Bending in front of the fridge, her legs looking long and perplexingly tanned for December, is Holly in a pair of denim shorts and a grey T-shirt, the epitome of casual-cool.

'Happy end of term!' I say to her with a smile. I'm feeling warm with the old holiday spirit, but more than that, I've felt less entirely suspicious of her since I saw her crying outside the sixth-form block last month. 'Hope you're doing all right now.'

But she doesn't return my warmth, and her nostrils flare, presumably at my audacity in even alluding to her moment of weakness. Fine, fine, fine.

'Brave of you to wear that skirt,' she says, casting a critical eye over my outfit.

I feel her taking in the way the stretchy jersey clings to the fat around my middle. Clearly my good vibes towards her are not going to be reciprocated. But I don't care. I just don't care what Holly thinks of me tonight. I don't have room to care. I only have room to look forward to seeing Joe.

'Thanks, Holly,' I say brightly, winking at her, before exiting the kitchen to dance with my friends who are waiting for me. Horrible Holly's going to have to try harder than that to dampen my mood tonight, the mean-spirited little sprite. I wonder if anyone's waiting for her to come back with a drink, or if she's so unnecessarily rude to people, she'll just end up hanging out alone all night, throwing side-eyes at everyone.

It feels good to be at a party and not continually checking the door to see if Joe's walking through it. It makes me feel like a chilled-out normal person who can just drink and dance with my friends. I know he'll be here eventually.

'I got here early so I could call things off with Oliver before the party,' Abi murmurs to me as we sit on the sofa after exhausting ourselves to Rihanna.

'What? Why?' I ask. This is certainly not what I was expecting to hear from someone who seems relatively relaxed and happy right now.

'I realized, after our conversation, I was never going to want to have sex with him. And that's important to him, you know? It's cool – we still really like each other. I mean, I'm here at his party aren't I? But I just feel better now the pressure's off,' she says, smiling.

Huh. That seems like a cool, grown-up thing to do.

I smile back. 'Good for you.'

We clink our bottles together and sink back into the sofa, chilling out in companionable silence. It's only when I see Joe chatting to Oliver in the doorway of the living room that I realize *splayed casually on soft furnishings so that you have several chins* is not the most seductive position. I scramble to my feet and go over to greet him. I didn't even know he'd arrived . . . When did he get here? He doesn't seem to be making any effort to come and find me. I guess he doesn't know I'm already here.

'Hey,' I say, all low and soft and as seductively as I can. I snake an arm around his waist and kiss him on the cheek.

'Oh, hi,' he says, jumping back in surprise at my touch.

Why is he shocked to see me? It's probably just me. Chill out, Emily.

Oliver smiles at me. 'Abi told me you guys were—'

'I'm going to get another drink,' Joe interrupts, and he dashes off, calling back over his shoulder to ask if I want anything.

I just shake my head. He's so tense – he's talking to me like he doesn't know me very well. Something feels off. When Joe's disappeared into the kitchen, and it's just me and Oliver, some strange impulse compels me to surreptitiously lift the can of Red Stripe Joe left on the coffee table to see if it's empty. It's not.

OK. It's probably nothing. He probably just changed his mind about what he wanted to drink and went to get something else . . .

But when Joe comes back, he's holding a can of Red Stripe and, if I'm not mistaken, deliberately positions himself on the other side of Oliver. But maybe I am mistaken? Snap out of it, Emily. He did not just pretend to have to go to the kitchen to get away from you. He just wouldn't.

The hours tick by fairly uneventfully, but a shiver of suspicion has been set off in me. I'm watching all Joe's movements through the obsessive lens of *What does this mean?* – taking them all in, watching for signs. Signs of what? Signs, I suppose, that he either does or doesn't care about me. It feels like tearing the petals off a daisy.

*He loves me; he loves me not.*

Joe squeezes my hand fondly as he passes on his way to the bathroom (*he loves me*). Joe has still not kissed me (*he loves me not*). Joe keeps catching my eye and smiling at me (*he loves me*). Joe will not stand next to me for prolonged periods of time (*he loves me not*). Every time I think I've cracked it, he'll do something to make me change my mind. Part of me wants to grab him by the collar and shout, 'WHAT ARE YOU DOING? WHAT IS YOUR GAME HERE?' in his face until he spells it out to me, but obviously that would be decidedly un-chill, so I can't.

That's it. That's what I'll do. I'll switch off. I'll mentally check out. For one night only, I will stop thinking about him; I will stop caring about him; I will stop analysing his every move. I will go about the rest of the party as if he wasn't here. Fine.

I dance; I drink; I hang out with my friends. I try to let Joe slip out of my mind, which he doesn't, because I'm manufacturing the forgetting, meaning – ironically – he's always at the forefront of my mind. But still, at least I'm not constantly on the lookout for him. I don't care what he's doing. I'm hanging out with my friends. I'm playing it cool. I'm cool. My mind is constantly looking, but my eyes are determined to stay distracted.

After a solid couple of hours of ignoring Joe – in which I've given Abi a pep talk on why breaking up with Oliver was the right thing to do, made friends with some girl in a Joy Division T-shirt, mediated an argument between Ella and Sophia, and invented a new cocktail (the Bloody Emily) with some dudes in the kitchen – nature calls, and I set off in search of the bathroom.

Props to Oliver: this is a well-attended party. People are hanging out in every room; a few people are in the garden, even though it's cold. That said, I don't pass Joe as I make my way upstairs, and with a little twist of regret I wonder if he's already left. Would he really leave without saying goodbye to me? God, what a washout. This was meant to be a fun party for me, but I've spent the whole thing feeling kind of miserable. This was meant to be the first party that I officially attended with Joe, and instead I've spent it conspicuously separate from him. I hope he hasn't left already. Maybe there's still time for him to make up for being cold earlier.

As I'm washing my hands at the sink, I look out on to the small, well-manicured garden. I turn to grab a towel when something out there catches my eye. A couple locked together in a kiss. The guy's hand up the girl's shirt. My blood runs cold, but I can't take my eyes off the scene – I just have to make sure I'm seeing what I think I'm seeing. There's no doubt about it. There, in the garden, floodlit by the brilliant white light from the patio, is Joe. And Holly. Unmistakably.

I can barely breathe. It feels like my chest is being gripped by a huge, hot, iron fist. Don't cry, for God's sake. Just don't cry. I sit on the edge of the bath and zone out. But my trance is interrupted by someone banging on the door. I jump to my feet.

'OK, OK – I'm nearly done,' I call, my voice shaking so much, it doesn't even sound like me.

'Emily, is that you?' I realize it's Abi on the other side.

'Yeah, um . . . do you want to come in?'

'Not with you in there . . . Wouldn't that be a bit weird?' she asks.

'No – I need your opinion on something,' I say, looking once again out of the window to check they're still at it. I shudder. They are. I open the door, and Abi enters with trepidation.

'What's going on? I only wanted a wee,' she says.

'Look out the window, into the garden,' I tell her.

She leans on the sink for a moment, craning her neck to prove she's really looking. Then her eyes widen.

'Oh . . .' she says.

'Yeah.'

'Literally what the actual hell? What *is* this?' Abi's nostrils flare with fury.

'It's definitely him, isn't it?'

'Yeah,' Abi says, craning her neck again to get another look. 'It's definitely him, the absolute fool. And it's definitely Holly. I know by those stupid little shorts.'

'God. Why? Why does this have to happen to me? Why . . . can't things just work out right?'

Abi gives me a sympathetic look. 'This has *nothing* to do with you,' she says, grasping me by the shoulders.

'It feels like it does. It feels like this is about me,' I say, exasperated and, finally, on the point of bursting into tears.

'No. Emily. You wouldn't do this to someone, would you?'

'No, Jesus, no.' I shake my head as tears start rolling out of my eyes.

'And why not?'

'Because it's wrong? Obviously?' I say impatiently, brushing the tears away as gently as possible so I don't smudge my mascara.

'Right. You wouldn't want to hurt someone you cared about. This isn't your fault. This is their fault.'

Abi moves away from the window, and we perch ourselves side by side on the edge of the bathtub.

'It's just one kiss, maybe it doesn't mean anything . . .' I trail off.

Abi exhales loudly. 'Even if that's the case, look how it's made you feel!'

'I've thought about him every day for months on end. I wanted him so much! I don't just want to throw this all away now I've got it.'

'It seems like he's the one that's throwing it away. Which makes it very easy to see that he's not good enough for you in the first place.'

'But Horrible Holly! Why her?'

'I don't know. I would say he has bad taste in girls, but . . . he doesn't. You're a perfect treasure.'

'I don't feel like one right now. I feel like an ugly, unlovable mess.'

I'm not used to talking like this about myself. I want to be strong and kickass and assertive. How dare he put me in this position, where I'm blaming myself for being treated like this. But maybe it is my fault. Maybe everyone is right. Maybe if I wasn't fat, these things wouldn't happen to me. Maybe I would be easier to love. Maybe I wouldn't be as easy to hurt. Maybe I would be more valuable. Maybe I only have myself to blame. Maybe I should have bowed to the pressure years ago and gone on some crash diet.

'Emily, you are *not* an unlovable mess. Clearly, you've got something going for you, and that's the problem. Holly's always been jealous of you.'

'Jealous? Of me? What?' Why would Holly be jealous of me? Holly who's too mean to care what anyone thinks of her.

Holly who's much thinner and much prettier than me . . . The idea of Holly wanting anything I have is totally bizarre.

'Because you do so well at school without trying! Even when she tries, she doesn't get as good grades as you do. And she really cares about grades. If you don't do well, you just shrug it off and move on; you know it's just because you were having a bad day or hadn't revised or whatever. But Holly's always competing with you, whether you're competing or not.'

'Oh . . . well. I never thought my grades would be something that someone would be jealous of.' Abi's hypothesis sounds kind of absurd, but also . . . I can see it. I can totally see it.

'For real, they are. It's not all about guys and looks, you know. You saw how upset she was when she didn't get into the uni she wanted to go to. She really minds about that stuff.'

'And given she didn't like me anyway, she won't care how much I like Joe. Hurting me is just a bonus,' I say, slumping backwards into the empty bathtub.

'She doesn't even know you're with Joe, though – surely this is just a coincidence?'

'No. This is not a coincidence. She must have been planning this ever since she saw him outside school. He was waiting for me there one day last term, and she commented on how cute he was. Maybe if I'd gone for a less cute guy, she wouldn't have wanted to make out with him, and I wouldn't be here now. This is what I get for punching above my weight.'

Ugh. That expression. Somehow it always comes back to my weight. I sigh, sprawling pathetically in the tub. God, this is just horrible. I feel like I'm being turned inside out. I want to wail and throw myself at him asking what's going on. Or maybe I just want to wail . . .

We've been in here a while now, and the knocks on the bathroom door have become too insistent for Abi and me to ignore any longer. We're ushered out so people can use the toilet as intended rather than as a therapist's office.

I look at my watch. It's late, and there's not much party left in me, so I decide to call it a night and head home. I give Abi a hug and go downstairs, but just as I'm making my way to the front door (attempting a quick, quiet exit, not wanting to say goodbye to anyone else in case I burst into tears when I open my mouth), I feel a hand on my shoulder.

'You off?' Joe asks.

As if he cares. I turn around to face him. He's swaying slightly and his gaze is unfocused. Clearly he's been powering through those cans of Red Stripe. I notice pinky-brown lipstick smudges around his mouth. I'm glad I already spotted him and Holly, that I've already felt the sharpest bit of the pain, that I'm not finding out right this second.

'Yeah, I'm going home,' I say defiantly.

'Oh, cool. I didn't get to hang out with you much,' he says, looking at me intently like he's trying to figure out if I know or not.

And whose choice was that?

'You didn't really seem up for it,' I say.

'Oh. Sorry,' he says, leaving the words hanging there dully.

'Anyway. Bye.' I turn to leave.

Why isn't he trying to say goodbye properly? Why doesn't he try to stop me from leaving and say, 'Hey, let's do something fun soon.' I guess I'm really not top of his list of priorities tonight. As I go to pull the door closed behind me, I see him already meandering off towards Holly. She catches my eye and waves at me, her face twisted into the smug smile of victory.

It feels like the bottom has fallen out of my stomach.

# CHAPTER TWENTY

'What Have I Done to Deserve This?' –
Pet Shop Boys

Christmas is rubbish. You wait all year for it, and then it's a huge anticlimax. So far this year, it's been even worse than usual. I've woken up every morning of the holidays and managed about three seconds of awakeness before remembering that Joe is gone, and everything is rubbish, and I never deserved him in the first place. And now it's Boxing Day which is the most bleh day of them all.

There's been radio silence from Joe ever since the party a week ago. He's probably off with Holly, rolling around under the mistletoe. But I'm not contacting him. I thought my silence might prompt him into action, but no. Nothing. I don't know what I'd say to him; I just want to hear something from him. I want him back. I'll be normal, I promise; I won't be a weird stalking girlfriend; I won't mind if we have sex or not; I won't mind about anything. As long as I have him. As long as I've got someone incredibly fit and clever who gives me records and wants to talk about books; someone who says I'm cute or beautiful or whatever he wants to call me.

The only thing that's making this holiday in any way bearable (apart from my dad's cooking and a constant flow of Cadbury Roses) is the fact Katie is back from Manchester for a few days. It's a welcome distraction, but it has also made me feel quite down. I tell her all about Joe, and I can tell she feels sorry for me over what happened with Holly, which I just hate. Even though I would feel sorry for me too. I hate that I'm someone you would pity, I hate that such pathetic things happen to me, and I hate that they get me down so much. I should be able to bounce back from this in no time, but here I am, all sad and moping and going through the box of Roses looking for the strawberry creams as if that's going to solve all my problems.

I've made a 'Heartbroken Moping' playlist that's getting heavy rotation right now (highlights include 'These Days' by Nico, 'Go Your Own Way' by Fleetwood Mac, and Robyn's unbeatable 'With Every Heartbeat'). It's one of my best – I almost want to share it with Joe, but, of course, that would be weird and the wrong thing to do. It's filtering through my headphones as I'm lying on the sofa, absent-mindedly opening the shiny red chocolate wrapper with one hand while holding a copy of Patti Smith's *Just Kids* in the other, unwilling to take my eyes off her magical prose, when in comes my mum to disturb the peace.

'Eat too many of those and you'll always be Fatty Smith, never Patti Smith,' she says, casting a glance over me and simultaneously managing to weaponize both of the fairly innocuous items in my chubby hands against me.

I sit up and just stare at Mum in shocked silence for a moment. She's already switched on the TV; she's not even interested in my response. It's like she doesn't expect me to have one. Or it's not important. It's only important for her to say what she wants about my body whenever she wants to say it. What am I meant to say? A petty part of my brain flares up to tell me how annoying it is that Katie has gone out for the evening and isn't here to witness this! She thinks I'm exaggerating whenever I complain to her about Mum having a go at me because of my weight, but I absolutely am not. It's the banality of it that gets me. Why? What's the point? What's the goal in saying stuff like this to your child? It feels like she just sees an opportunity to make a mean comment and takes it.

'What's your point?' I say, finally. It comes out stilted, of course.

'Just that you can't afford to put on any more weight. Just because it's Christmas, that's no excuse,' she replies, not taking her eyes off the TV.

'Actually, I would say there's no better excuse than the birth of our Lord and Saviour Jesus Christ,' I say. 'Also, can you please just absolutely lay off me about this? Surely you're bored of it by now?'

Finally she bothers to look at me.

'No, Emily – I am not bored of having an interest in my daughter's health and well-being. I'll take care of you even if you won't take care of yourself.'

I can feel myself vibrating with rage.

'You have to stop! Just stop! You're making it impossible for me to have a relationship with you!' I shout, louder than I probably should.

I leap off the sofa, storm out of the room and pound up the stairs, making the most of my weight as I stomp on every step. Up in my room, I slam the door behind me for effect and go to retreat under the duvet, but first I trip over a coat I've left on the floor. My general rage at the world is peaking right now. I am not in the wrong here. I am entirely in the right. But I can't stew in my righteous anger for long; a sheepish knock on my bedroom door interrupts my rage. Dad pushes the door open and picks his way across my floordrobe.

'You two need to go easier on each other,' he says, sitting down on my bed. He takes his glasses off and leans his head against the wall. I bet it's boring for him to be surrounded by this constant anger.

'Each other? She's my mum! She's the grown-up – *she's*

the one who's meant to behave responsibly!' I cry. How can he possibly be on her side in this? What even is her side?

'I know, I know. And you're not wrong – her obsession with your weight is getting in the way of your relationship,' he says.

Yeah, I think. Not just our relationship, but *my* relationship. 'So?' I say.

'So . . . you've got something that she'll never have. Something that she might never learn: you like yourself. You don't lie awake at night worrying about your body. You're not going to waste hours and hundreds of pounds on fad diets. And no one can take that away from you. Your mum is a brilliant woman. So sharp, so intelligent, capable of so much love. It's just a shame that this fixation on her weight seems to have run away with itself.' He shakes his head sadly. 'Maybe in time she'll learn something from you. Just be more gentle.'

A shadow appears at the bottom of my doorframe, and the floorboard creaks.

'Can I come in?' Mum sniffles from outside the door.

'I'll leave you to it,' Dad says and sidles out of the room, squeezing my mum's arm as he passes her.

She appears to be carrying a peace offering: a pink fondant fancy on a little floral-patterned plate. She comes in and sits next to me on the bed, putting the cake on my side table. We sit in silence for a while, sadness and fury whipping silently between us, neither of us daring to breathe too loudly in case it's taken to mean we cracked first.

'I'm sorry for upsetting you,' Mum says, finally. A tear drops silently down her cheek.

It breaks my heart to see her cry. 'I want to say it's OK, because I can tell you're upset too, but it's not OK. I can't keep dealing with this from you . . .' I trail off.

'No, you shouldn't have to. I just . . .' She looks upwards, seemingly trying to conjure the right words. 'I just worry about you, Emily. About your health. About your happiness.'

'Well, we all die someday. But for real, there's more to health than weight, and I don't think being thin has ever protected someone from death,' I say, attempting a laugh.

'That's not something to joke about, Emily! All I'm saying is I've never been able to be happy with my body the way it is, that's all.'

'But I'm not you, Mum,' I say. I try to sound soothing rather than confrontational. 'I'm me. We're different people. We were always going to have different experiences of the world, even if our bodies were the same. And I'm perfectly happy. In fact . . . it's getting kind of hard to tell what is my weight holding me back, and what is just me holding *myself* back . . . you know? Because I've internalized the things you say to me. I listen to what you tell me.'

'What things?' she asks, looking confused.

I realize that she doesn't fully understand the impact that her words have on me. They don't just roll off me like water off a duck's back. They burrow deep inside my mind.

'Well . . . for one thing, telling me I'll never get a boyfriend unless I lose weight. That just means that I'm super grateful if someone shows me attention, whether they're right for me or not. Whether they treat me nicely or not,' I say. And finally, the tears that I managed to bite back when I was fighting with Mum earlier begin to roll down my face.

'Oh, treasure,' she says. She looks genuinely crestfallen. 'Who's been making you feel bad?'

'It's OK. I don't really want to talk about it right now,' I say, and although I'm still crying, my mum's concern has warmed my cold heart enough to muster a smile too. 'But thanks for asking.'

'Emily . . .' She sighs, resting her head on my shoulder – an act more affectionate than any I've felt from her since I was really little. 'I just don't want you looking back on this part of your life and wishing you'd done more, had more fun,' she says. 'Not let your body hold you back.'

'I have enough fun, Mum. Don't worry about that,' I say.

But she's not listening; she's still buried in her own fears. Her face clouds over.

'It's not my body that's holding me back. I think it's

more of a problem that people *tell me* my body should hold me back.'

'I could never shake the feeling that your dad was a total fluke,' she says.

'What does that mean?' OK, so we're clearly not talking about my life any more.

'I mean . . . he's just so lovely and kind, and he was always so handsome, and he'd do anything for me, and for you and your sister. And I have never really been able to believe my luck. I always felt like I was hiding in plain sight, that he hadn't properly realized I was . . .' She trails off. She closes her eyes, apparently trying to muster the right word. Or perhaps bring herself to say it. '*Bigger*, you know? Or it was just a matter of time before he was going to tell me I needed to lose weight.'

'So . . . even though you had evidence that someone lovely and kind and, bleurgh, "handsome" wanted to marry you, you still thought it was some kind of weird oversight on his part? That he'd wake up one day and realize what a terrible mistake he had made in marrying you, all because you're fat?' I ask, incredulously.

My mum flinches. 'Don't use words like that, Emily,' she says.

I forget that it's still such an inflammatory word to so many people. Maybe in that way I'm lucky.

Mum shrugs. 'When you put it like that, I suppose it

does sound stupid, but it's always made sense to me.'

I realize it makes sense to me too, in a horrible sort of way. My poor mum. Struggling under the weight not of herself but a culture that trained her to second-guess every kindness, to eye every advance with suspicion.

I sigh. 'I don't want to fight with you, Mum.'

'Oh, me neither, treasure. You're such a good girl. Such a clever girl,' she says, stroking my hair. 'Maybe it's time I gave up on the mad diets. I don't think I can really keep it up much longer anyway. If they really worked, they'd have worked by now.'

'That . . . sounds like a good plan,' I say. I don't bother mentioning that I saw her eating the leftover turkey skin on Christmas Day.

Mum pats my leg, gets up and leaves the room, turning around at the doorway to give me a conciliatory smile, before closing the door quietly behind her. I pick up my fondant fancy and nibble on it as I click around the internet, zoning out, letting my eyes glaze over. Facebook. Twitter. Tumblr. I'm listening to my Hairpins record that Joe gave me, a tangible thing that proves he cared about me. I don't want to think about anything. I just want to feel right again. The way I did before I met Joe.

There's another knock at my bedroom door. Who is it now? The three wise men?

'What now?' I groan.

'It's me,' Katie says as she slinks in and closes the door behind her.

'I've made up with Mum, so you don't need to tell me to be nice to her.'

'I wasn't going to, I promise.'

'Oh.'

'I just wanted to chat. I realized I never replied to the email you sent me when you were in a bad mood that time. I kept thinking about how to reply, and then eventually I thought it would be too late, and it would be weird, and maybe you didn't really want my advice anyway – maybe you just wanted to let off steam.'

'Yeah, that's what it was,' I say, thinking back to the email where I inarticulately articulated all my fears about my body holding me back and ruining my romantic life. 'It's fine. I don't really need any help. Things are different now.'

'Sure?'

I pause. I swallow. I'm not sure. But I'm also not sure what Katie can say that'll make a difference.

'I can't even remember what I wrote . . .' I say, trying to sound like it can't have been that important anyway.

'I've got it here,' Katie says. She comes to sit next to me on the bed as she scrolls back through her inbox.

I don't have time to stop her before she begins the cringe-inducing task of reading it aloud.

Hi, K,

Sorry I didn't pick up. I'm just in this weird place at the moment with Joe. There's this nagging feeling that my body is getting in the way of things. Like it doesn't matter how cool *I* am about it, it's just . . . a problem. It's like the THING that I'm pinning everything on, and it'll just be there hovering about causing trouble forever, no matter what I feel about it!!!

Anyway, don't know why I'm complaining to you – will ring you back soon.

Love you!!

Emily

'See?' I say breezily, although I'm red with cringe at laying my vulnerabilities out like that. And also because it strikes me that I've done such a good job at burying them over the past few months – burying all my feelings just so I could have some kind of relationship with Joe. 'Just a little rant.'

'Yeah . . . It's fine to talk about it though. Even if I don't, like, totally understand everything, I'm still your sister, and I still want you to be happy. And I still want to pass on my adult lady wisdom to you because it makes me feel important,' she says, smiling.

'OK – let's do it, if only to make you feel important.'

'Well, first, I know you don't like talking about your problems and stuff, so it's cool of you to acknowledge you were feeling something. And second, it feels like there are two answers to your central issue—'

'Which is what?' I cut her off, admittedly rudely, because I need to know she understands.

'Well . . . it sounds like you were basically asking if dating is going to be harder because you're bigger?'

'Yeah, basically. Also, you're allowed to say *fat*.'

'OK – I'll try. What I would have said, had I not rudely neglected to reply to your email in a timely fashion, is that our culture is generally misogynistic. So, all women get judged on their bodies according to, like, general dude standards. And general dude standards enforce thinness. So, yeah, more judgement is levelled at fat women, and this is the same in dating and romance as it is in the world as a whole.'

'Ugh! I knew it!' I say, overcome with a wave of

pessimism, rage and embarrassment all at once.

'BUT!' Katie says, raising a hand in an attempt to halt my tirade. 'Adolescence is the worst time. Boys can be awful at this age and totally motivated by peer pressure and weird, average standards that they haven't even bothered to think about, let alone question. They just want to do whatever their friends are doing; mock whatever their friends are mocking. Obviously some guys never grow out of this – and I would know, I've met a few of them – but I promise you, it will never be worse than it is now.'

'Really?' I say, even though this is pretty much what my aunt already told me, and I have no reason to doubt either of them.

'Really. I'm not saying it's guaranteed to be easy – that's partly to do with the people you have around you. Surrounding yourself with kind and interesting people and trying to meet people, guys and girls, who are decent and intelligent enough to at least be able to look critically at things like general dude standards, that's the best way of feeling more at ease about dating.'

'So, it's not like no one ever wants to date fat girls?'

'No. No way. I have cool adult lady friends of all sizes, and even though men can be terrible, and often are, my friends who are plus size, fat, whatever, seem to be dating constantly. I swear!'

'Based on information I have gathered throughout my lifetime regarding your behaviour and speech habits, you appear to be telling the truth . . .'

'I am! And what's more, none of my friends are you. You're already this cool at seventeen! Just think what you'll be like when you've lived properly, doing your own things in the world outside school and Mum and Dad's house. I am not worried about you at all. It might be hard, and you might have to wade through more crap than I have, but you're so cool and fun and no-nonsense, and you are going to have a great time when you fly the nest.' She clasps me by the shoulders and shakes me like a rag doll with a force that underscores how sincerely she means it.

'I just feel like . . .' I sigh and tilt my head towards the ceiling. 'Like maybe I just don't deserve someone good? Someone that really wants me? That the best I can hope for is just . . . someone.'

'No,' Katie says in an absolutely positively decisive tone. 'I am going to tell you this now, without any hesitation, and even though we have different bodies and different problems, I know this is true: *never settle*.' She shakes me a bit more. 'Do not allow into your world someone who thinks you're second best, who thinks your body is a temporary "problem" that you're going to solve, who puts you down in *any* way.'

She's looking at me intensely now. 'Em, I know it might

be hard to believe now, especially if you want to date guys, who are almost uniformly jerks at your age and possibly beyond. But there really are people out there who will make you feel magical and beloved and special and important. I'm just sorry you don't know that already. Compromise on where to go for dinner. Compromise on what movie to see. Compromise on how to balance your work–life relationship. But don't *ever* compromise on the level of love, attention and enthusiasm you know you deserve. You'll feel it when you have it. You'll feel like you're being loved wholeheartedly for *who* you are. And you'll always know when someone is incapable of giving that to you because they cannot deal with your body. Do. Not. Compromise. If someone is making you feel any less than magical, you're probably compromising.'

And I hear her. Really hear her. I had always thought Joe was the one compromising. A cute, cool guy who wanted to date me, a fat girl, must be the one compromising, right? . . . But what if it's actually me? What if I were confident enough to know that I could date someone who's proud of me, proud of all the great things about me? Who wants to show me off to his friends. Who wants everyone to know we're together because it's so exciting and important to him. It's like a bad optical illusion: once you see how it works, you can't go back to seeing it in the fun, dizzying, disorienting way that you could before.

Now that I can see that everything Joe did was designed to keep me at arm's length, to keep me a secret, I can't go back to writing it off as a misunderstanding. Second-guessing him, making excuses for him.

I clear my throat awkwardly after a too-long silence. 'Thank you for this,' I say. 'I have a lot to think about.'

'Any time, Em. I'll leave you to it, then, shall I?' Katie says, slinking off the bed. 'I hope I've helped.'

And as if by magic, the title track of my Hairpins record comes on, whispering to me through the vinyl, through the needle, through the speakers, into my room.

> *But you never wanted me around*
> *Thought you could pick me up and put me down*
> *Make me feel like this was never real*
> *Like I'm no big deal.*

I lie back on my bed, thinking, slowly nibbling away at the remnants of the little pink cake Mum brought me earlier. And then I've thought too much and just want to get out of my own head. I get up and go downstairs to discover that Katie and Dad have both gone to bed while I ruminated in my room. But Mum's still up, watching the same Victoria Wood rerun that they show every Christmas.

I stick my head around the living-room door. 'Mum . . .'

'Yes?'

'Do you want to watch something?' I ask.

She smiles. 'I haven't seen *Gentlemen Prefer Blondes* in a while . . .'

'Me neither,' I lie, reminded of one of the first times I ever hung out with Joe. But watching it lying here on the sofa with my mum – finally, weirdly at peace with each other – feels better than any date with Joe ever did.

# CHAPTER
# TWENTY-ONE

'No More Tears (Enough Is Enough)' –
Donna Summer and Barbra Streisand

I wake up on the morning of New Year's Eve feeling like there's a lead weight on my chest. This is how it's felt every day since The Bad Party. I can't wait for this year to be over. I just wish things had gone differently with Joe.

A group of us are going to Ella's for a 'Select Gathering' while her parents are at a friend's party. I'm just grateful to have something to take my mind off Joe. I've already decided on a black velvet dress with a Bardot neckline and some chunky-heeled ankle boots. It's a relief not to be dressing for Joe tonight. Not to be second-guessing what makes me look cutest to him, what's most likely to make him fancy me. I thought I was above that, but, hey, turns out I'm not. Anyway, there's no point wondering about him now. He's all in the past, I think to myself. The thought feels like a knife twisting in my chest. I miss him already. But I am definitely ready for a clean slate.

Because it's a special occasion, we have prosecco. It makes

us feel extremely adult. We put on a playlist I've made of particularly banging party bangers. We play drinking games. There are only ten of us (Select Gathering, remember?) but it feels just right. I'm kind of numb right now. It's hard to accept that Joe would rather have Holly than me. It's hard to accept that Joe was ashamed of me, didn't want me to meet his friends, didn't want to be seen with me, didn't want anyone to know we were anything other than mates. But I'm trying to accept it. He was meant to be here tonight, but obviously after not speaking to him for a couple of weeks, there was no question of casually dropping him a line to see if he still wanted to 'hang out' on New Year's Eve.

We've settled into a sprawled mess across Ella's living room. Couples and friends reclining comfortably on soft furnishings, basking in the warm glow of the fire. Camila begins telling me about how she went over to Ryan's house on Boxing Day and how it felt like a Big Moment in their relationship for her to be at a family gathering . . . but I don't catch the whole story, because I think I hear the doorbell ring. At first, I wonder if it's just the music. But then an insistent knocking breaks our cosy peace.

'A few people said they were coming post-midnight, but I thought everyone we were expecting was here already,' Ella says, scanning the room with a confused expression as though trying to figure out where the gap is. 'Clearly not.'

As Ella bounds off to the front door, I pour myself another glass of prosecco. Nibble a few more crisps. It's New Year's Eve after all. When she returns, she looks intensely uncomfortable.

'Emily . . . Joe's here,' she says, biting her lip. 'To see you.'

'To see me?' I ask incredulously.

'I can tell him to leave if you want,' she offers.

I know she would if I asked. But am I ready to do that?

'No, it's OK. I'll talk to him.' Clearly I'm not quite ready to tell him to leave just yet.

And then I see him, slowly and awkwardly making his way into the room behind her.

'Hey, Emily,' he says.

I scramble to my feet and brush the crisp crumbs off myself as gracefully as I can.

'Hello, Joe. What can I do for you?' I ask. I sound like a middle-aged man. Real smooth.

'I . . . I wanted to talk to you. To explain things. I couldn't wait any longer. I'm sorry for crashing the party, but I just needed to see you,' he says, lowering his voice and looking at me very seriously.

Talking quietly can only ever half work when there's a group of girls trying to eavesdrop on your conversation. They will catch everything. Over Joe's shoulder, I see Abi raise her eyebrows at me as if to wordlessly say, *'Go!'* They can definitely hear us.

We creak up the stairs to find somewhere private to talk. We settle on Ella's sister's bedroom, a riot of pink and pop stars and trinkets and glitter. Joe sits down on the bed. I sit next to him. We sit in silence for a few seconds before he puts his hand on mine. I don't pull away. He's so soft and warm – how could I pull away from that? We look at each other, but neither of us says anything. Silence.

'So . . . what did you want to say to me?' I finally ask.

But instead of answering, he just looks into my eyes, cups his hand around the nape of my neck and fondly strokes the back of my hair with his thumb. Then he leans forward and kisses me. This is everything I want. Joe. Back. My heart beats fast, and I let myself go, and everything feels like it's swirling around me. This is everything I want. But it just doesn't feel right.

'Would you do that downstairs?' I ask abruptly, pulling away from him. 'In front of people? Would you do that in a restaurant? On the street? In the cinema, before the lights go down? Would you tell your friends you're seeing me? How would you feel if you had to show them a picture of me?' I can't keep it in – it's all pouring out of me, and I can't stop it.

Joe shifts uncomfortably next to me on the bed and

buries his face in his hands. The spell is broken. Well, that certainly bodes well for his reply.

'Is this about Holly?' he asks, looking shifty. 'Because if it is, I'm sorry. It was a stupid mistake. I shouldn't have done it, and I've regretted it constantly ever since.'

'No, it's not about Holly, but that didn't help me feel good about myself.' What's the point in holding back now? Might as well tell him the truth.

'I'm sorry, Emily . . . It's not like that . . .' he says.

But in that moment, I know for sure that it is like that. And the crushing realization that I can't pretend any more washes over me like rain.

'Please don't deny it. If you deny it, it just makes me feel like I can't trust you,' I say.

'Why do I have to demonstrate it all the time? I like you. Isn't that enough? Why do I have to perform it for other people?'

And, just like that, I start to second-guess myself. Maybe he's right. Why isn't that enough? He's all I want. And now he's here, and he wants me. Can't that just be enough? Why does he have to be making out with me in front of the whole world? What if this is my only chance at love and romance and sex? What if no one wants me ever again? That could happen. It's not totally out of the question . . . I feel alert with panic and indecision. And the indecision gives way to a softening. I'm all ready to cave and melt and be grateful. I even open my mouth to speak, to say, *Yes, yes – it's enough. It's OK. Let's just be in love.*

'Maybe . . . I guess . . .' is what I say instead. I chew the skin on my lip and shift around on the bed. 'I just wish . . .'

'What? You wish what?' Joe's looking at me with a kind of dread. Like he doesn't really want me to answer.

But I hear a voice in my head. A wise, sisterly kind of voice. A voice that has advice just for me. Advice I wanted to ignore – advice I wanted to believe didn't apply to me – but, my God, it really, really does. *Compromise. Compromise. Compromise.* If I start compromising now, I'll never stop.

'You know what? No,' I say, not really knowing for sure where I want to go from here, but knowing all the same that it's where I have to start. I have to start with 'no'. 'I wish you would treat me better. That's what I wish, but I know you can't give me that. I deserve better than this. I deserve better than you. I deserve more, and I'm happy to wait for it. I was crazy about you. I feel like I dreamed about you for nights and nights. I was always so excited to see you, always so scared that every time would be the last time, and you would just disappear.' I know I sound completely wild at this point, but if I don't say this stuff now, then maybe I never will. 'And I just fancied you so much, and I had so much time for you, and wanted to get to know you, and wanted to know everything about you.'

I look him in the eyes. 'When I kissed you that first time, I really meant it. That was the real me, showing you what I really meant and what I really wanted, even though it was embarrassing for me because, come on, who does that out of the blue? And I was so painfully ashamed of it because I thought you would just not want to see me again and you would be totally freaked out by it, but it turned out you weren't. And that was so amazing. The fact you said you had feelings for me too was just so completely amazing . . .'

I stop for a second because it's painful for me to remember that. To have had that conversation with him, for him to have said those things, to have given me so much hope and so much excitement. I take a deep breath.

'But those feelings you say you have . . . what do they mean for me? What do they give me? Because it seems like your feelings just add up to nothing because you're at war with them. I can't be with someone who finds it so hard to care about me.'

As I speak, Joe has stopped looking me in the eye. He's looking around the room, at the floor, at the posters of pop stars on Ella's little sister's wall, at his sleeves, at his hands — anywhere but at me.

'I'm sorry,' he says.

'Yeah. I'm sure you are. Because I would have been the best girlfriend in the world if you'd given me a chance. I would have done just about anything for you,' I say. Jesus, why can't I stop baring my damn soul to this guy? 'This isn't about Holly. But if it was, I think that would be OK, to be honest. It's about all the ways you treat me like I'm not important, like I'm not special, like you can pick me up and put me down and play with my feelings and pretend you don't have any feelings when someone's around to see them. You don't need to say it out loud. I can tell why it is . . .' I trail off. I need to say it out loud. I need to. But acknowledging this feels like something I can't come back from. Naming the problem is like acknowledging the elephant in the room. And here, the elephant is me.

'I know it's because of my body,' I finally say very slowly. 'And I know you fancy me. I know you would have slept with me if I hadn't freaked out after hearing those rumours you were super experienced. But, Jesus, the way you can't even kiss me in public. The way you tried to make sure none of your guy friends would ever suspect we were dating. The way you go out of your way to avoid even standing near me at a party in case I try to do something as disgusting as hold your hand . . . I now totally realize that's why you only wanted me to come to the shop when no one else was around – why you told me to message you rather than dropping in while you were there—'

'I really fancy you! I always have!' Joe protests, his voice shrill. 'But . . . you know what guys are like. They can be total dicks. About, like, dating and sex and stuff.'

'I don't doubt that you fancy me, or that you think I'm great. But you need to chill the hell out about what other people think of you dating a fat girl. And I don't think you can.'

'So . . . that's it?' he asks.

Is that it? Do I mean it? Is that really it?

'Yes,' I say.

'Wow,' he replies. He's shaking his head in disbelief, like I've said something completely absurd.

'I like you, Joe. I like you so much. But I like me more. And you're not capable of being proud of me, of being excited to be with me, and I really believe that there's someone out there who is. Maybe not right here, right now – maybe not even in Croydon. But I'm not scared any more. I'm not scared of being left behind, of being the odd one out. I'm just scared of letting myself believe it's normal to be treated like I'm an embarrassment. I can't do that to myself. I can't let myself think it's normal for someone to be ashamed of me. Because then it becomes normal. And I deserve better.'

Joe laughs, but it sounds defensive. 'I'm not *that* bad . . .'

'But . . . you're not that great, either. I felt like you were such a catch, like you were so much better than me, like I didn't deserve you. But you're not.'

Oh God, my mouth is totally running away with me now. But honestly, after the pain of the whole Holly drama, I can't help twisting the knife a little. Anyway, it's all true.

'You're just an average guy, who does average-guy stuff, like reading average-guy books and caring about average-guy opinions.'

He can't look me in the eye. At least he's not protesting any more.

'And I think we've spent enough time on this, to be honest,' I say. 'I'm going to hang out with my friends now, and I would assume you have somewhere else to be. I'm sure Holly's having a party tonight.'

I thought what I wanted more than anything was Joe, but I think what I *really* wanted was to be sure of myself.

And now I am.

As I descend the stairs to see Joe out, I realize it's only a few minutes until midnight. Joe will walk out into the darkness, alone, and I will be here in the warm glow of my friends.

And it feels good.

At midnight, we all crowd into the garden, and Ella and Sophia let off fireworks. Ella kisses Sophia. Camila kisses Ryan. Abi hugs me tightly. It would have been nice to have someone to kiss at midnight, for the first time. It would definitely have been nice to have someone as cute as Joe to kiss at midnight. But it's even better to be going into the new year as a new me. I know it sounds cheesy, but it really feels like it. An Emily who can stand her ground.

An Emily who knows what she's worth.

By one o'clock, we're dancing to 80s music in the living room. I'm the only one that hears the doorbell over the sound of 'Tainted Love', so I go to answer it, even though I'm pretty sure we're not expecting anyone else.

I peer cautiously round the door, half wondering if it will be Joe. If he's come back to try and win me over . . .

'Hey,' the guy says.

It's not Joe.

'I'm Ravi. I'm a friend of Ryan's. I was at another party, but it got kind of boring, so he said I should come and hang out with you guys. If that's all right with you?'

My jaw drops and kind of hangs open. I can't reply.

He's the cutest guy I've ever seen.

# Acknowledgements

Thank you first and foremost to Rachel Petty, without whom this book would literally not exist, not one word. Thank you to Sarah Hughes for making this book 1000% better than I ever could have done alone. Thank you to Annemarie Blumenhagen for introducing me to Siobhan O'Neill at WME and to Siobhan in turn for agreeing to be my patient and kind agent. Thank you to Simran Sandhu for your absolutely invaluable cheerleading and insight. Thank you to Kat McKenna and Sabina Maharjan for marketing and publicising this book like the absolute dreams that you are. Thank you to the great authors Alice Slater and Will Dean for listening to me, giving me support and reminding me I am a real writer. Thank you to Jenny Tighe and Beth John for being there every step of the way. Thank you to Rachel Vale and Kristina Mordokhovitch for creating the perfect cover. Thank you to Dan Barker for such a truly extensive list of things I don't know where to start. Thank you to my family, but especially my parents, for the endless encouragement, enthusiasm and for fostering a love of reading. Thank you to Paul Haworth, the artist and the person, for everything, always.

# Author's Note

Hello reader!

I am not Emily, I am Bethany, and I wrote this book. With that being said, a lot of the things that Emily experiences and feels are things that I experienced and felt, not just as a 17-year-old but into my twenties, right up to the present day. In some ways, it doesn't matter how far you come with your own personal story of self-acceptance, it can still feel hard to live in a world that demonises and vilifies fat bodies. No amount of self-love can change that.

Between writing *No Big Deal* and the book being published, I was struck with a bit of fear that the way the story plays out will reinforce an anxiety among fat girls that they are unloveable, that their partners are always ashamed of them, that they are doomed to an unhappy romantic life. But what I really wanted to say is that romance will come and go, but the great love of your life is yourself. That figuring out your limits and boundaries and priorities will enable you to have better relationships, even if sometimes that means walking away from them when your approaches and desires and levels of commitment aren't compatible. This is something that everyone, whatever their size or age, would benefit from.

Emily is incredibly confident in herself, but if you're not quite there yet, I found that the most powerful and meaningful way to embrace my body was to find a community of people who looked like me. Feeling like the odd one out is so incredibly hard and confusing, and realising that's not the case at all can be life-altering. Seeing people who look like me, who understand my struggles, who can relate to my experiences, who can advise from a place of real knowledge and empathy, has been really wonderful for me. We don't always have to agree or have had exactly the same experiences, but just knowing I'm not the only fat person in the world is a good place to start.

Another thing I've found really healing in my life is to not surround myself with people who think that diets and weight loss are interesting conversational topics. They simply aren't. Removing these kinds of conversations from my life makes me feel more secure in social situations, and leaves more room for talking about more stimulating things with more interesting people. You're allowed to choose what kind of conversations you want to participate in, and it's okay to politely decline to talk about topics that make you uncomfortable. It can be as simple as saying 'That's not something I do' or 'That's not really an important part of my life'.

The final thing that allowed me to have a good relationship with my body is having an honest relationship with it. I touch it, I engage with it, I look at it, I let it be seen and photographed from lots of different angles rather than trying to preserve an illusion of it that, ultimately, doesn't help me to see myself realistically. Real, meaningful self-acceptance has to be based on truth rather than illusion, and you can't truly accept a body you don't accept you have.

You are allowed to be fat. You are allowed to have the body you've been blessed with right now. You don't have to change if you don't want to. You're in good company.

I hope you found something useful in this book, that it made you feel a little bit more comfortable in the world, but either way, I'm really honoured you took the time to read it.

Thank you,
Bethany